CW01511002

Standish Cope has been writing for over fifteen years and has authored a radio play, a stage play, and an audio-story for the 'Green Curtain' Theatre Company, poetry, and a host of peer-reviewed articles in complementary medicine. Standish Cope's preferred genre is the historical novel and *The Rift* novella is his first endeavour in this regard.

I dedicate *The Rift* to Anthony and Dymphna, my late parents, and the many thousands of victims, mostly African, sacrificed during Britain's last colonial war.

Standish Cope

The Rift

AUSTIN MACAULEY PUBLISHERS™

LONDON * CAMBRIDGE * NEW YORK * SHARJAH

A CIP catalogue record for this title is available from the British Library.

ISBN 9781035828258 (Paperback)
ISBN 9781035828265 (ePub e-book)

www.austinmacauley.com

First Published 2023
Austin Macauley Publishers Ltd®
1 Canada Square
Canary Wharf
London
E14 5AA

I should like to thank my friend, mentor, poet, and writer, Lydia Fulleylove.

Chapter One
Isabel The Train Journey, 4 June 1952

Nairobi Railway Station in early morning. Sounds of a busy Asian market all around us: shouts, gesticulations and gushes of steam from the engine, and white-turbaned men wearing what looks like jodhpurs pushing carts laden with fruit, flowers, coconuts and all kinds of exotic produce. Porters calling out to us complete the cacophony.

'*Bwana na Memsab*! You want porter? Cheap price!'

I look across the carriage to Ted and he shakes his head.

'Don't worry, we'll manage.'

He begins to wrestle our bags off the overhead storage racks, perspiring heavily as he does so.

'Let me give you a hand,' I say, and he passes the smaller cases to me below.

Wafting through the window, I can smell sandalwood, jasmine and mixed spices as lines of rainbow-coloured women in saris walk up and down the platform selling bananas, nuts and fruit to the weary travellers leaning from the windows.

Ted is craning his neck outside the carriage window hoping to see signs of Juma, our designated houseboy, who has been sent on ahead to meet us from Nyeri. As we clamber out of our compartment, I can see a tall, black, sinewy, well-dressed man wearing a cotton khaki suit coming towards us with a sack truck. He is grinning from ear to ear through his splendidly white teeth.

'*Karibuni, Bwana na Memsab,* welcome to Nairobi!' He says enthusiastically.

'*Hujambo,* Juma!' Ted replies to his greeting.

'*Habari ya safari,* how was your journey, *Bwana na Memsab*?' Juma asks.

'*Safari njema,* good, Juma,' Ted replies.

9

'*Gari ni hapa, Bwana. Kuja,* come, the car is here!' Juma beckons us out of the station once he has piled our entire luggage on his capacious cart.

'*Asante sana*, thank you, Juma,' Ted replies, and we follow in Juma's wake through the busy throng of arriving passengers and their welcoming parties.

Juma's luggage cart seems to weave effortlessly through clusters of waiting passengers, hawkers and over-burdened porters, as we jostle our way forward through human and animal traffic. The British high commissioner's car is waiting for us with his immaculately turned out driver in his Sikh turban and neatly turned, handlebar moustaches.

'Welcome, Mr and Mrs Edwards. The high commissioner asked me to bring you to his residence in the staff car. My name is Kapil,' he says.

'Thank you, Kapil,' Ted says as we climb in while Juma stows our luggage and makes his own way to the commissioner's residence.

I can almost feel the colonial tones of Isak Dinesen in Kapil's warm and gracious greeting towards Ted and me. The Mercedes saloon winds its way through a string of Asian *dukas,* shops, balancing mountains of multi-coloured plastics alongside serried bolts of vivid velvet and cotton sari-making materials.

Soon we're leaving the busy streets of Nairobi, and we begin to see tethered goats and wicker cages filled with chickens, and clusters of *watoto,* children playing games on the broken pavements, or chasing each other across hazardous streets shouting greetings to passers-by. Gradually, the dust of the city gives way to the sparse white clouds of the Highlands in the middle distance beckoning us on to further mysteries in this exciting continent of Africa.

The Mercedes proceeds smoothly up a sisal and palm tree-lined avenue towards the high commissioner's residence in Muthaiga with its English lawn and exotic shrubbery. The only detail that strikes me so far about this journey is the presence of army vehicles on the main thoroughfares, and a small cluster of armed African policemen, *askaris,* outside the main post office. I wonder what that's all about.

When the car comes to a stop, Kapil begins unloading our luggage on to the driveway while the commissioner's deputy comes out to meet us.

'Welcome Mr and Mrs Stephens. My name's Charles Steel and I will be accompanying you up country to your new appointment in Nyeri, Rift Valley Province.'

'Ah, hello, Charles! This is my wife, Isabel, and do call me Edward in future.'

'Pleased to meet you both,' Charles responds.

Charles appears to be a dapper young man in his mid-30s, wearing a smart beige cotton suit, sandals and white socks. He seems eager to befriend us and be our guide and mentor as we begin to make sense of the cultural ways and mannerisms of the up country "White Highlanders", about which I have read a little in the press. The high commissioner and his wife are delightfully charming and we enjoy a light luncheon with them, chicken and cucumber sandwiches, before we depart for "Kingston Farm", Nyeri, our new home, feeling cheerful and refreshed.

Kapil has kindly stowed all our suitcases, hat boxes and miscellaneous parcels in the back of the army Land Rover, and we have a jerry can of water on the back in case of a breakdown or overheated radiator. The high commissioner and his wife wave us off as we leave the manicured gardens of their residence and head for the savannah plains of the Rift Valley, and I'm filled with a spirit of hope and adventure.

The first thing I notice after we leave behind the few tar macadam roads in Nairobi is the nature of the native housing. There seems to be row upon row and mile upon mile of mud huts made from mud and wattle, woven with palm fronds and secured with hemp string. In between are open, running drains. I remark on this to Ted.

'What do you expect, Izzy? They're hardly civilised, you know,' he responds.

'It must be terribly hard for them, having to live in such abject squalor,' I reply.

'Well, Izzy, what you'll soon discover about the natives in Kenya is that they're too idle to do anything about their situation.'

I don't feel up to challenging Ted's opinion, so just kept absorbing all these amazing scenes and smells around us. I reflect that in some ways, these rudimentary huts are a lot more salubrious than the hovels piled haphazardly along narrow, evil-smelling lanes in Nairobi, where illness and disease seem rife.

In the end, I suppose, I can't be judgemental about Ted. After all, my national schooling in Dublin taught me all I know about Africa that could be summed up in the strange idyll of small, black, wiry natives canoeing up crocodile-infested rivers living on bananas and coconuts. Neither a truthful nor edifying image, I suspect.

What we do both take pleasure from, as we progress along the red sandstone, pot-holed country roads however, is the sight of long-horned cattle, giraffe, zebras and gazelle grazing on the gently undulating savannah bordering the long road to Nyeri.

'We're now entering the province of the Masai tribe, Izzy, so do look out for the ochre-painted warriors and their large herds of cattle,' Ted says, looking quite enthusiastic for a change. We have been travelling through the undulating savannah when I call out to Ted:

'Stop!' I shout. 'Someone's hurt.'

Edward slows the car and pulls into the side of the road. He hasn't noticed him at all. Standing there is a tall, young, lean, red and black Masai warrior dressed in a long, brown blood-spattered robe, and holding a wood and iron spear in his left, uninjured, hand. His right arm hangs limply by his side and his upper body is covered in caked and congealed blood, with folds of exposed flesh attracting a swarm of flies.

'*Wenda wapi*, where are you going?' Edward asks the young warrior.

'*Napenda hospitali, Bwana,* I need hospital, *Bwana,*' he replies. Edward gets out of the Land Rover and helps the young warrior into the back seat, but can't persuade him to part with his spear, so we complete our journey to Nyeri hospital with the man's spear protruding from the back window, while Ted and I look at each other from time to time marvelling at the quiet, stoic endurance of this young Masai warrior.

Chapter Two
Isabel Arriving at Kingston Farm

Driving up towards Kingston Farm, set amidst the purple, forested Mount Kenya range ahead of us, I notice a native settlement of thatched huts in relatively good repair. Among and around the huts are fields which seem replete with maize and beans. Perhaps this is their staple, I muse. Then I hear the *watoto*, lithe African children running up the drive shouting "*wazungu, wazungu*, British, British", in increasingly excited tones. We both smile.

As we pull into the drive at Kingston Farm, our colonial style house with terrace, Juma, our houseboy, and Elena, his wife, come out to greet us in their best white and black regalia. How nice to see Juma again, and his wife, whom I've not met before.

'*Karibuni*, welcome, *Bwana na Memsab. Habari ya safari*, how was your journey?' They chorus.

'*Safari ndefu, lakini njema, Juma na Elena,* long but good,' Ted replies on our behalf.

Juma and Elena help with our luggage and escort us into our new African home. I can't wait to have a good look around, but we are both exhausted from our arduous trip and just want to drink, eat and sleep. Elena seems to have an easy and genuine manner and I feel sure we will get along well. And I can plainly see that Ted already has an easy rapport and respect for Juma, our houseboy.

After we've eaten, Ted and I look at each other across the dining table and listen to the growing chorus of tree frogs singing around the forest perimeter. It feels lovely to be together in our new home in Kenya, and I try to put aside some of my niggling fears triggered by the number of troops and policemen I've seen in Nairobi today.

In the morning, I begin my exploration of the house and farm which has taken the toll of termites, tropical monsoons and the lack of a female presence, I suspect, judging from the state of dilapidation of the furniture and fittings. The house is square, with a Georgian-style portico, verandas, and ivy-clad windows looking out over to the stunning Rift Valley on one side and Mount Kenya on the other.

What impresses me most about our new home are the hardwood floors, which will look superb with a bit of wax floor polish, in due course. The downstairs drawing room has some beautiful, hardwood furniture in the colonial style, with lovely woven carpets which resemble richly-woven tapestries. They look like Kashmir to me.

After we've unpacked our belongings, I go downstairs to meet our gardener, Eliud. He's a tall and wiry young man with a mischievous grin and tribal markings on both his cheeks. A Luo by tribe, Ted tells me.

'*Karibu,* welcome, *Memsab*,' he says.

'*Asante sana*, thank you, Eliud,' I reply.

'I am your gardener, *Memsab*,' he continues.

'Well, Eliud, I look forward to you showing me the garden, or is it *shamba* you call it in Swahili?' I ask.

'*Vizuri sana, Memsab*, you speak good Swahili!' He laughs.

'*Kuja, Memsab*, let me show you,' he beckons me outside.

'You lead the way.' And I follow Eliud outside.

As I follow in the wake of Eliud's guided tour of our garden, he stops often and points to a growing crop of vegetables and says,

'*Nyanya*, tomatoes, *Memsab*.'

'*Nyana*?' I say.

'*Hapana*, no, *Memsab*. *Nya-nya*,' he laughs and enunciates with a big grin.

'*Nya-nya*?' I proffer.

'*Ndio,* yes, *Memsab*. *Nyanya*,' he says.

'*Nyanya*,' I repeat.

'*Ndio kabissa nzuri,* yes, very good, *Memsab*,' Eliud congratulates me.

In this manner, Eliud shows me all over our kitchen garden, and not only do I have a fair idea what vegetables he is growing on our behalf, but I also begin to learn the Kiswahili words for most of our domestic crops at Kingston Farm, which is a fascinating education for me.

Before we part company, I say to Eliud, 'Eliud, *asante sana* for showing me over our *shamba*. Can you also tell me the name that the local people give to the snow-capped mountain over there?' I point north of Kingston Farm.

'*Ndio, Memsab*. We call our sacred mountain *Kere Nyaga*. It is home of chief God of Kikuyu tribe: *Ngai*.'

Kere Nyaga, I rehearse, as I contemplate the splendour of our sacred mountain horizon.

'I work now, *Memsab. Kwaheri*, goodbye,' Eliud says as he saunters his way back up the path carrying his large, *jembe*, or hoe, over his shoulder.

'*Kwaheri*,' I call after him and make my way back to the house.

Chapter Three
Eliud's Story, September 1952

Mama taught me well. She show me to make soil rich by adding manure and planting small bushes to stop rain washing soil away. I am good at looking after hens and we have lots of eggs to sell for paraffin, and school fees for my brothers and sisters. I am happy to meet my wife, Rachel, who is also good farmer. She looks after our *shamba* very well.

Now I work at Kingston Farm, house of *Bwana na Memsab* Stephens. *Bwana* pay me five shillings every week to look after their *shamba*.

First planting season at *Bwana's* house, I show *Memsab* how we plant *mahindi na maharagwe,* maize and beans. *Memsab* tell me they do not grow these things in her big town over the seas. Now she wants me to plant lettuces and small, black *calabashes*. Rachel never plants these on our *shamba*. But I do know how to plant *nyanya,* tomatoes, which *Bwana na Memsab* like very much. They eat *mahindi*, maize, which is good.

I remember a talk I have with *Memsab* when I first come to Kingston Farm. *Memsab* ask me about *Mau*. I tell her.

'Many of my tribe are joining *Mau, Memsab*.'

'Why is that, Eliud?' *Memsab* ask.

'It is because *wazungu* have taken our ancestral lands, *Memsab*.'

'Will you join the *Mau*, Eliud?'

'No, *Memsab*, I am happy here, with you and *Bwana* Stephens. I like my job, and you are kind, *Memsab.*'

'I am pleased that you and your family are happy here, Eliud. Please tell me if there is anything that you need.'

'*Ndio*, yes, *Memsab. Wewe ni hisani,* you are very kind, *Memsab*.'

'Don't mention it, Eliud.'

Memsab is very kind lady. I do not want to tell her that I am hearing more bad things about *Mau Mau*. Kikuyu tribe are taking *Gethathi* oath to curse *wazungu* and send them from our land forever. I am worried about my family and my job and I will not swear *Mau Mau Gethathi*. Then, one day, *kijana*, a young man comes to Kingston Farm, the house of *Bwana na Memsab* Stephens. He is tall, ragged and bony. I can see he is troubled.

'*Tunatoka kijana*, where are you from?' I ask.

'*Natoka*, Nakuru, *Kaka*,' he replies.

'*Jina laka*, what's your name?'

'*Jina*, Bado, *Kaka*.'

'*Kwa nini wewe hapa*, why have you come here?'

'*Nataka ku-timika, Kaka*, I need job,' he says.

'I can't help you, Bado. You must go from here.'

'*Tafadhali, Kaka*, please, Uncle! *Wataka ku-fua mimi, Kaka*. They will kill me!' He says, shaking.

'*Nani*, who'll kill you?' I ask.

'*Mau, Kaka*.'

I see he's hungry, thirsty and has fear for his life.

'*Ku-kaa*, sit here, and tell me your story, Bado.'

Bado start to shake when he tells me his story.

'They came in night with fire torches and *pangas*, machetes, *Kaka*. I cannot sleep. I hear them in our village. I try to wake my mother and father, and my brothers and sisters. We cry from fear. They shout at us and mock us. I can smell burning and screaming around me. They put fire to our hut. We run out and they cut us with their *pangas*. I don't stop. I keep running and running.

'I can still hear the sounds of my mother and sisters crying for mercy. There is none.' Bado is crying now.

'*Tafadhali, Kaka*. Help me, I beg you, Uncle.'

So this is *Mau Mau*, I am thinking and I hold out my hand to Bado.

'*Njoo*, come. Let us talk to *Memsab na Bwana* Stephens.'

Bado is still shaking when I bring him to *Memsab*. She listens to him and is very kind.

When we are in kitchen eating *posho*, Bado tell us about his family.

'My father work for British East African Railways as ticket collector, 3rd class. It is good job and he pay for food and school fees. Then, one moon ago, *Mau Mau* come to our village and say we must swear *Gethathi*, oath against *wazungu.* We say *hapana,* no and *Mau Mau* leave village at night. They say we will all suffer for not taking *Gethathi.* You know rest of my story, *Kaka.*'

When Bado finish speaking, *Memsab* Stephens is quiet. She says she will speak with *Bwana na* Robertson family and ask if they can offer Bado job. He has tears of happiness. *Memsab kuwa hisani,* she has kind heart. She will do it.

Chapter Four
Munthu's Story, October 1952

The sun is already showing his face behind *Kere Nyaga*. I love this time when I can see and hear our *wanawake,* women, walking with their *watoto* on their backs on the way to market in Nakuru. Some elders among them have already gathered in the centre of the market square where they chew tobacco and tell their stories to the *watoto,* grandchildren, who listen to every word.

I smell fires and see women pounding maize in preparation for making *posho,* boiled maize, in their blackened cooking pots. The men of our tribe sit in small groups smoking, while the boys run off to herd goats on the edge of the village. Wambui, my wife, beckons me.

'*Baba, kuja hapa,* father, come here. Sam and Liza are fighting again.'

'*Wasiwasi,* don't worry, I can see them.'

'*Mama, Mama.* Sam has eaten more than his share,' Liza cried.

'Liza, Sam, stop it. Both of you. How can your mother feed us if you eat everything she has brought to sell?'

'Try and catch me,' Liza taunts Sam.

'*Mama,* it's not fair,' Sam cries.

We all stop in our tracks as we hear a high pitched scream from the market square and I see a crowd of people surrounding a *kijana,* youth, waving his arms around. The *wazee,* elders, are also leaving the square hurriedly.

'Wambui, take care of the children while I go and find out what's happening over there.'

As I approach the centre of the surging crowd, I see and hear a troubled youth.

'*Wa-rafikiangu!* Friends! A miracle!' He shouts.

'*Mimi ku-ganga.* I've been healed.'

A huge crowd has gathered around him, looking at him with doubt and confusion in their eyes. A woman in the crowd calls out.

'*Nani ku-ganga,* who healed you, *kijana*?'

'*Ma-babu,* my spirit ancestors, *Mama*.'

Others question or challenge him boldly, and the boy becomes more animated.

'*Ku-sikiliza!* Listen! There is a prophecy.'

'What prophecy?' Someone shouts.

'There will be a war between black and white. Between brother and brother. Father and son.'

A little way to my left, I see an *mzungu* in a khaki uniform writing in his notebook and looking at the *kijana* with suspicion.

'We will rise up against the *wazungu,* but we will be crushed.'

'What are you talking about, you mad boy?' Someone jeers.

'Yes, he's crazy,' someone else concurs.

Others are not so sure and listen attentively to what the boy has to say.

'The struggle will divide brother from brother. Family from family. We will be destroyed. We must not fight.'

I follow the *mzungu* with my eyes. He hurries to the police station where I see another *mzungu* officer coming towards the crowd with a troop of *askaris* with guns and batons.

'Ayeee! *Kusaidia!* Help! Help me!'

I see the crowd surrounding the screaming boy to protect him from the *wazungu* officers and the *askaris*. The armed officers and *askaris* now face the crowd with their guns raised. The *kijana* stops screaming and there is silence in the crowd. Suddenly, some Kikuyu men rush towards the *askaris*. I am afraid for them.

The *mzungu* officer with a pistol shouts out, 'Stop! Go back or we shoot!'

The young men curse the *askaris* and move forward. Then I hear the *mzungu* officer shout, 'Aim, ready, fire!'

Their guns explode and my Kikuyu countrymen are cut down like maize in my *shamba*. They keep on falling as the *askaris* keep shooting. Screaming women and children are running away as fast as their legs can carry them. Then there is a terrible silence as I see the bodies of my tribe, women and children scattered everywhere lying in their own spilled blood.

My heart is heavy as I run back to Wambui and the children.

'*Tuende! Haraka!* Hurry! Let's go from here before the *wazungu* come and create more bloodshed.'

Chapter Five
Dinner at Kingston Farm, 20 October 1952

Sunset has come quickly over the White Highlands, leaving the orange-ochre glow of the equatorial sun which has cast its final rays over the gleaming *Lenana* Glacier on Mount Kenya. All around Kingston Farm, the orchestration of cicadas and tree frogs can be heard, embellished by the sounds of the kitchen staff putting the finishing touches to the sumptuous dinner being prepared for Judge and Mrs Isabel Stephens and their guests.

Isabel is wearing an attractive, white-ivory silk dress with a set of pearls, setting off her auburn hair, and Edward is in his best dinner jacket and black bow tie.

'So, Charles, tell me about the recent Muthaiga polo match?' Edward asked.

'I'm sorry you weren't there to witness it, Ted. But, as you may have heard by now, we outclassed the opposition by the sheer skills of our teamwork and the fitness of our Argentinian ponies. They didn't stand a chance and to cap it all...'

'Come on, gentlemen, I think us ladies have heard enough about the polo match by now, let's rather hear about the *Mau Mau* uprising...'

'Why don't you and the ladies retire to the lounge, Izzy?' Edward prompts.

'But we want to hear about the recent Kikuyu uprising, don't we, ladies?' Isabel responds.

'I don't think we need to heighten anxieties among our ladies, do we, dear?' Edward says pointedly.

'Actually, Ted, I think we...'

'Please, Izzy,' Edward insists.

Isabel looks accusingly at Ted, and takes in the two ladies with her eyes and gestures, as Mrs Steel and Mrs Anderson get up to leave the dining room table. A brief and awkward silence follows.

'So, Ted, what you make of the recent declaration of the State of Emergency?' Chief Inspector Mike Anderson asks.

'Frankly, Mike, I think it's only a small minority of agitators who need to be taught a lesson and more...'

'I think you underestimate the problem, Ted,' Mike responds. 'And in my view...

'I think Mike's right, Ted,' says Charles. 'The *Mau Mau* is getting large numbers of recruits through their oath-taking ceremonies and...'

'If you want my opinion, I would round-up the ring leaders, try and charge them with sedition and conspiracy, which might serve as an example to the others,' Edward interjects.

'If we did that, Ted,' interrupts Mike, 'there's a risk we'd make martyrs of them and...'

'So what? We've got the manpower and resources to quell any kind of rebellion they care to organise, though I doubt they're capable of that,' replies Edward.

'I wouldn't underestimate these extremists, Ted,' says Charles. 'From what I hear...'

'You're on the right track there, Charles,' says Mike. 'My intelligence officers tell me that since the last riot in Nakuru, where there were a few casualties, *Mau Mau* recruitment has rocketed.'

'The point is,' responds Ted, 'they're a small minority of an ignorant and docile population, Mike, and they don't have the support of other tribes...'

'The trouble is, Ted,' says Mike, 'they're being led by ruthless rebels like "General China" and Field Marshal Dedan Kimathi who've taken up defensive positions in the forests around Mount Kenya and the Aberdares.'

'Well, Mike, I'm sure you and your intelligence officers are smart and organised enough to mount a pre-emptive attack on these ill-equipped rebels, aren't you?'

'You make it sound like child's play, Ted,' says Mike. 'It's a lot more...'

'It's quite simple. I assure you,' Ted interrupts.

'I think, first, we need to ask what's behind the *Mau Mau's* strategy,' interjects Charles.

'What strategy? Do you seriously believe they have one?' Ted responds.

'The Kikuyu are calling for Land and Freedom, that's what's behind it all, Ted,' says Charles.

'Well, it's too bad. They're incapable of running this colony, let alone mounting a credible rebellion against us,' Ted replies.

'But I hear there's talk of introducing "internment without trial" for the Kikuyu. What do you think of that, Ted?' Mike asks.

'As a judge, I'm reluctant to dispense with "trial by jury", but I'm prepared to look at that possibility should the need arise,' Ted replies.

'However,' says Mike. 'I fear that we may be sowing the seeds of our own demise if we do that, and…'

'What you have to understand, Mike, is that we have to extirpate these terrorists from the "White Highlands" or we'll never be able to sleep in peace and enjoy the lives we've created for ourselves here,' Ted responds.

'I think Ted's right, though, Mike. We've no choice but to nip this rebellion in the bud, and use whatever means at our disposal,' Charles says finally.

At this break in the conversation, Juma comes into the dining room and asks, 'More whisky, *Bwana*?'

Juma places a carafe of whisky and a jug of water on the dining room table.

'*Asante sana*, Juma. That'll be all for tonight.'

'*Nzuri usiku, Bwana*,' Juma responds.

'Good night,' says Edward.

Chapter Six
Edward's Story Kingston Farm,
5 November 1952

It begins with a blood-curdling scream that wakes our entire household. I stick my hand under the pillow and feel for the hardness of the revolver. 'It's there, thank God,' and throwing the bedcovers off, I search with my feet to find my slippers.

'What's wrong, Ted?' Isabel asks anxiously as she stirs from her restless sleep, heavy with child.

'I'm just going to find out. Stay here, Izzy. Check to see your revolver's there,' I instruct.

Izzy grabs my left arm before I stand up to go.

'Careful, darling,' she says as I rush towards the bedroom door. In my haste, I almost run into Elena on the way out. Cleo and Rex are barking furiously and rushing at every door.

'*Gani!* What is it, Elena?'

'*Bwana, haraka!* Come quickly. They've killed Eliud.'

'*Haraka! Tuende!* Hurry! Let's go,' I reply.

I follow Elena, bounding down the stairs after her. Rushing from the house, I enter the servant's quarters. As I approach the gardener's hut, I'm greeted by sounds of keening women, and raised, angry voices. Pushing my way through the throng of people, I enter Eliud's low-ceilinged room.

Slumped over the bloody and bespattered body of Eliud is Rachel, his wife, weeping hysterically. Mary and Joseph cling to their mother's meagre, tear-stained clothing in abject grief, shock and tears.

'Who did this?' I shout above the din.

A stunned silence greets my cry. No one moves. Juma, who is comforting Rachel, speaks out, 'It was *Mau Mau, Bwana*. They did this.'

'How do you know?' I ask.

'I found a paper, *Bwana*,' Juma replies.

Juma hands me a badly crumpled and scrawled piece of paper. On it are written the words of the "*Mau Mau Gethathi,* oath".

We will not rest until all wazungu *have left our land. We swear this* Gethathi *on pain of death. If you do not support us, you will also die.* Ithaka na Wiyathi! *Land and Freedom!*

'They will pay for this,' I mutter to myself.

I feel sickened and exposed. The only *mzungu*, Briton, present among this incongruous gathering is me. I look around slowly, and as I do so, the faces of my servants stare at me with dull incomprehension and resignation. Before I turn to go, I say to Juma.

'Stay with Rachel and the children. I'm going to call Chief Inspector Anderson.'

'*Ndio, Bwana.*'

Stuffing the revolver in my dressing gown pocket, I leave the room abruptly. When I return to the bedroom, I find Isabel in her dressing gown sitting on the edge of our bed holding her revolver while Elena is telling her about what's happened.

Izzy reaches out her hand to me and I clasp it saying, 'It's all right, Izzy. We'll find and hang the culprits. I promise you.'

'It must have been horrible, Ted. Eliud was such a lovely man. How awful for Rachel, Joseph and Mary, too,' Isabel replies.

'I'm going to call Anderson. Stay here with Elena. I won't be long,' I say as I stride out of the bedroom and make my way down to the telephone in the hall.

'Hello, Judge Stephens here. Get me Chief Inspector Anderson, please.'

There's a pause.

'Hello, Ted. What's up?' Anderson asks.

'They've murdered Eliud,' I say.

'Who has?' Anderson asks.

'The *Mau Mau*,' I reply.

'I'll be there with a force as soon as I can, Ted. Stand by,' Anderson says.

I replace the receiver, check the ammunition in my revolver, and walk slowly upstairs trembling with shock at what I've witnessed this bloody night. As I climb the frayed carpet stairs, I begin to reflect on the fact that the "White

Highlands" are no longer a safe place to raise and care for my family. The risks are becoming too great and the benefits of a comfortable colonial life too meagre to weigh against them.

As I reach the landing and look through an east-facing window, the ochre-pink rays of the African dawn are appearing between the three peaks of Mount Kenya, the sacred home of *Ngai*, the powerful god of the Kikuyu. How can these wretched Neolithic people ever hope to be an educated, self-governing nation? It will all end in blood and sacrifice, like their ancestors before them, I reflect bitterly.

Chapter Seven
Munthu Aberdare Forest, December 1952

'Let me go, you devils,' I scream as a *Mau Mau* warrior twists his *panga* into my back.

'Kill the bastard,' someone shouts in my ear and spits.

'Yes, kill him if he doesn't swear *Gethathi*.'

'Wait,' the leader's voice resounds ahead of me. 'First he must serve us.'

I look up at the *Mau Mau* chief with a dishevelled beard and matted red-black hair. His eyes are like darting spears.

'Come here, *tai tai*, or I'll have you butchered like a dog.'

I'm pushed forward by the stabbing *panga* between my shoulder blades. The pain is so bad; I stumble and fall at his feet. He spits again.

'Get up, *tai tai*, and hear your punishment.'

I stand up slowly and look at this fearsome man.

'General China,' someone calls. 'Give him look-out's job.'

'*Ndio kabisa*, yes, indeed,' General China sneers at me.

'Because you refused *Gethathi*, *tai tai,* you must help us kill the *wazungu* farmers.'

Sweat begins to pour from me now.

'But they are farmers like me, *mzee*,' I stammer.

'When we have killed the *wazungu*, then you will swear the *Gethathi*. After that, we may spare you and your family.'

'Must I do this, "General China"?'

'You must, or die like a dog, *tai tai*.'

'*Ndio*, General,' I say, turn and walk away shaking with fear.

'You must keep watch for us from the edge of the forest, *tai tai*. Make no mistake. We'll come when the moon is full.'

As I walk away from "General China", his comrades' eyes burn into me like embers from an angry fire.

Now the moon is full. I wait until nightfall and watch servants return to their huts after serving the *wazungu* family with dinner. My stomach is turning like a roasted pig on a fire. I light my torch and wave it above my head. "General China" signals back to me. They come now. I see them move towards the farm house and surround it.

At a signal from "General China", they break the windows with their *pangas* and throw their lighted torches inside. They go inside. I hear shouts and screams, and then all is quiet. I am very sad because the Robertson family were farmers and good *wazungu*. They were my neighbours in Nakuru.

Slowly, I make my way back to the forest and am greeted by "General China". He's standing with a group of his warriors with their bloodied *pangas*. They're laughing and smiling at me, holding some spoils from the raid. "General China" speaks:

'So *tai tai* has now become one of us! You are welcome among us as a fellow comrade and freedom fighter, Munthu. *Ithaka na Wiyathi!* Land and Freedom! It has been a good day's work. Come and celebrate with us.'

I stand there but cannot speak. At last, I find the words.

'"General China", I am honoured by your invitation, but first I must tell my family where I will be going.'

'*Tuende sasa*, go now, but return soon, comrade. *Safari njema*, safe journey.'

'*Salama tu,* peace be with you, General.'

As I walk back into the concealing thickness of the undergrowth and the now obscured moon, my heart is heavy with the knowledge that I'm now a fugitive caught between the evil deeds of the *Mau Mau* and the vengeance of the *mzungu* security forces. I fear that Wambui, Eliza and Sam will all suffer because of my actions, and I realise that they won't understand the path I've got to follow against my will.

Descending the slope of the mountain, I remember the words of my spirit guide at my initiation. '*Kijana*, Munthu, you have been chosen to protect your peoples' ancestral lands. To keep them safe from the *kiengere*, the pink frogs who would steal it from us.'

Before I can help myself, I say, '*Na kusudia*, I will, *Mzee.*'

Now this is my fate, if God wills it.

Chapter Eight
Bwana Robert is Born Kingston Farm, Nyeri, 10 December 1952

Driving recklessly along the laterite road from the Nyeri Court House to Kitale that evening in mid-December, having issued eviction notices on all the Kikuyu "poll tax" resisters, I fear the backlash of the Kikuyu tribes following the trial and imprisonment of Jomo Kenyatta, their leader. Also I'm so preoccupied with thoughts of how Izzy's labour is going; I nearly end up in the thorn bushes skirting its edge.

Skidding into the gravel driveway, I leap out of the car and run up to the front door. As I open it, I smell the disinfectant and carbolic soap penetrating the air. Cantering up the stairs two at a time, I enter our bedroom expectantly. Izzy is lying propped up in the bed glowing and dishevelled. By her right hand side is a crib, with a baby lying fast asleep. I can hardly believe my eyes.

'That's incredible, my darling! How are mother and baby?' I ask.

'I'm exhausted but he's fine. And he's sleeping now, thank God,' Izzy replies.

'A boy. Wonderful!' I exclaim.

'Ted, what shall we call him?' Izzy asks.

'We agreed on "Robert", didn't we, after my father?' I reply.

'Why don't you hold him, so?' Isabel suggests.

I approach the cradle, pull back the covers from the tightly swaddled baby and pick him up gingerly, holding him close to my chest. As I hold this frail, sallow-looking boy with minute dark hairs forming on his fragile head, I have a momentary recollection of feelings I had towards Izzy when we talked of having children soon after I received news of my posting to Africa. I recall her words as we were sitting on a bench in St Stephen's Green, Dublin, sometime in early March 1951.

'I'm not sure about children, Ted, to be honest with you.'

'And why's that, Izzy?'

'Well, with you going off to Africa and all, I'm not sure it's such a good idea at this stage.'

'At least I've a secure and well-paid post with good prospects in the Colonial Legal Service.'

'It's not that, Ted, it's…'

'It's what, Izzy?'

'It's just that I don't feel it'll be a safe place to start a family, you know and…'

'You've no need to fear matters on that account, Izzy, as I have it on good authority that the maternity hospitals in Nairobi are of an excellent standard.'

'Really?'

'Well, yes, of course.'

'Well…in that case, I feel a little more reassured, Ted,' Izzy replied without conviction.

At the time, I thought nothing more of the conversation, but when we fell out shortly after that, Izzy went off to London to stay with her cousin, Moira, for a few weeks; I began to suspect something else was going on.

I remember the argument we had just before she left:

'Why is it that you're always pushing me away, Izzy? I thought we were committed to each other?'

"The thing is, Ted, we're always arguing nowadays, and it's wearing me out, and if I'm honest…"

'Well, it takes two to argue, Izzy, and…'

'You're always in the right, aren't you, Ted, and I hate your possessiveness. I feel like I'm like some kind of prize…'

'I love you, Izzy, and I just want to see more of you, that's all.'

'Can't you see, Ted, I need more time to think about things, and you're not….'

'Why, what's nagging you, Izzy, for heaven's sake?'

'If only you'd listen, Ted. I've been telling for weeks now that I've been offered a modelling contract with *Vogue* magazine in London and I want to take it.'

'What's more important to you, Izzy? You're modelling career or our relationship, for God's sake?'

'Well, when you put it like that, Ted, I'd have to say my career.'

'Do you really mean that after all that we've been through together?'

'Yes, I'm afraid I do, Ted.'

'I can't believe this is happening to us. I really can't.'

'I'm sorry, Ted, I truly am.'

I was crestfallen and hurt beyond words at the time and I didn't hear from Izzy for a few weeks until I received a letter from her with a London postmark, which I've kept.

But now, as I'm holding our beautiful child, I just breathe deeply as something in me seems to soften and melt. Very fleetingly, all my fears and suspicions give way to suffusing and unanticipated warmth. Izzy looks on radiantly at this picture of Robert and I embraced in this new dawn of life and promise.

Isabel

The night before Robert was born, the African stars stood bright and still in the firmament. I was elated and at the same time sad that I couldn't fully welcome him into the world as our son. The guilt I felt then has stayed with me since. It's a kind of bitter-sweet feeling which it's hard for me to shake, and although I regret my foolhardy moment with Francesco nine months ago, I welcome this precious boy into our lives with joy. And one of the most poignant memories for me tonight has been hearing our servants and local villagers sing, dance and play the *ngoma,* drums.

This native music has always been precious to me from the time I heard my parents sing the Irish ballads, with Da on the fiddle and Ma singing at the piano. I also fondly remember the times when Ted and I were happy enough to sing our operatic arias, like *Nessum dorma* or *Libiamo* from *La Traviata.* Yet this music of Africa is stunningly different.

It's got exciting rhythms which I've never heard before, and watching the warriors weave in and out of the circle to the chanting and ululations of the women is truly inspiring. Above all, I marvel at the way the *watoto,* children, mimic the warriors, hopping in and out of the dance circle like colourful birds of paradise.

Chapter Nine
Munthu Nakuru, January 1953

I stand before Wambui, my hands and clothes torn from running through the forest. She stares at me with unblinking eyes as if I'm an apparition. Breathing heavily, she steps forward and embraces me warmly.

'Munthu, where have you been?'

I begin weeping into her neck, scenting its acrid sweet smell.

'They forced me, Wambui. I had no choice.'

'What've you done?' Wambui's eyes search mine.

I struggle for honourable words in my shame.

'*Wa-kifua Bwana na Memsab*, they killed the Robertsons. '

'*Nani?* Who?'

'*Mau Mau.*'

'*Hapana.* No! How could you let them?' Wambui screams in disbelief.

'The *Mau Mau* said they would kill us, like they did our neighbours, if I refused to help.'

'But they were good *wazungu*, Munthu.'

'*Ndio, ni kujua.* Yes, I know,' I shout defensively.

Wambui's arms hold me tightly.

'*Wasiwasi*, don't worry. We'll go with you.'

'*Hapana!* No! You can't follow me. The security forces will hunt me down like a dog.'

'*Sisi njoo sasa*, we must come with you.'

'*Hapana kabisa*, not at all. Go back to your father's home. And take the children.'

'*Hapana.* No, we can't leave you.'

'*Tu lazima*, you must. *Sasa. Haraka*, now, hurry.'

33

Wambui relaxes her grip around my shoulders and slips to her knees, crying pitifully.

'*Tafadhali,* Munthu, don't leave us.'

I bend down and raise her to my eyes.

'*Ni ahadi*, Wambui, I promise I will come back to you as soon as the struggle for *Ithaka na Wiyathi*, Land and Freedom, is over. Let me say *kwaheri,* goodbye, to our children before I go.'

Wambui holds me tightly as we approach our hut.

'Sam, Liza. *Kuja hapa. Haraka*! Come here. Hurry! *Baba* is calling you,' says Wambui.

Liza is first to come out, rubbing her eyes from the daylight and smoke of cooking pots. She rushes up to me.

'*Baba, una fanya nini,* what is it?'

Before I can reply, Sam, a year younger than Liza, throws himself at me, and I catch him in my arms.

'*Baba. Wenda wapi*? Father, where are you going?'

Liza and Sam wrestle with each other for my embraces. I smell their sweet coconut-scented hair mixed with the smoke of cooking pots.

'I must go to the forest. The *wazungu* security forces are hunting me. Listen to your mother now. She is taking you to her parents in Nakuru. You'll be safe there.'

'*Lakini, Baba*, but, Dad,' Liza begins to shake and cry, and Sam joins in.

'*Hodari wawana.* Be brave, my son and daughter. I will return soon. *Ni ahadi*, I promise.'

As I stand up to go, all three of them embrace me.

'*Na-kusali Ngai na wababu,* I pray the ancestors keep you safe until we meet again,' I say.

I turn away and go off to collect my special hunting knife, *panga* and some necessities for the trip. In a short while, Wambui comes back with a small parcel of dried fish, bananas and a gourd of water for me to take on the journey.

'*Njoo*, let me give you this *Gethiito*, charm of protection,' Wambui says, as she removes one of her own cowrie necklaces and places it around my neck.

'*Asante sana, mke, na Salama*, thank you, and peace be with you, wife,' I say gently.

'*Safari njema, na salama, mume,* safe journey, and peace be with you, husband,' Wambui replies with a sweet embrace.

As I turn my back on our home and *shamba,* I have a bad feeling that I may never see my family again.

Chapter Ten
Sacrifice, 26 March 1953

A gibbous moon flits between the scudding clouds over Mount Kenya forest as though revealing the dire intentions of General China and his comrades. The *Mau Mau* have concealed the smoke from their location by running long, hollowed out bamboo poles to carry the smoke hundreds of yards away. They have spent the previous night overseeing a *Gethatha,* oathing ceremony, in which a handful of reluctant Kikuyu have been "persuaded" of the merits of the struggle for *Ithaka na Wiyathi,* Land and Freedom.

Those reckless enough to refuse the *Gethathi,* Oath sleep on in their *nyumbani,* huts, blissfully unaware of the punishing carnage about to befall them. General China, as always, wants to give his fighters a pep talk before the Operation:

'Well, comrades. I have only one thing to say to you before you sacrifice these weak and cowardly people for refusing *Gethathi.* Be thorough in your work and spare no one.'

His words are greeted with assenting cries, *'Ndio, patana,* we agree, General!'

As General China's comrades emerge from the forest before dawn, they begin to fan out like a deadly spider's web preparing for its hapless prey. The warriors carry spears, bows and arrows, *pangas,* machetes, lighted torches, and a random collection of guns captured from their frequent ambushes of *askaris* in the surrounding valleys.

At a prearranged signal, they all descend on the sleeping villagers like a horde of deadly hornets, setting fire to all the huts and killing any living being that stirs. Soon the terrain is littered with the hideous sights of men, women and children being hacked to death with *pangas,* burning huts, overturned pots and gourds; the smoke of singed hair and flesh and the incessant cries for mercy which go unheeded.

When all seventy-four Kikuyu men, women and children lie dead, all that can be heard above the sounds of unquenched fires in the former village is the bleating of distressed goats that are soon to be corralled, killed and prepared for a sacrificial feast.

Before General China's comrades leave the remains of the smouldering village that was *Lari,* he decides to remind them of the path they have chosen. Speaking with strings of precious stones and metals in his left hand, the spoils of some of his victims, he raises his right arm, holding a *panga* and speaks, 'Comrades, I congratulate you on your thorough work today. Let this be an example to all those Kikuyu who dishonour *Ithaka na Wiyathi,* Land and Freedom, by not swearing our *Gethathi.* For those who don't learn from their cowardice, may what we have done today be a lesson to them.'

'*Ku-patana, ku-patana,* we agree, we agree,' his loyal comrades chant in response.

The freedom-fighters then depart the blackened and smouldering remains of *Lari* village.

Eventually, when news of the "*Lari* Massacre" reaches the outside world, a perspicacious and talented journalist called James Cameron writes:

The Rift Valley has revealed that the main body of resistance to Mau Mau is more than ever now the decent Kikuyu who have suffered most grievously and violently for the excess of both sides. (The Age, December 1953)

Predictably, the martyrs of *Lari* never read his accolade. However, the security forces, with their loyal *askaris,* were swift to respond to this outrage by perpetrating another massacre of innocents and suspected *Mau Mau* terrorists that claimed double the number of lives in the troubled Rift Valley Province.

Chapter Eleven
Edward Nyeri Court House, 27 March 1953

I'm standing fully robed outside the main courtroom wearing my judge's regalia, and addressing Chief Inspector Mike Anderson.

'I want you to start the evictions straight away, Mike,' I say.

'Surely we'll need permission from the chief justice first, Edward?' Anderson asks.

'No, we don't. Having refused to pay the Crown the poll tax, and having had due notice, these squatters have surrendered their right of appeal. Just get on with it,' I reply.

'As you command, Justice Edwards,' Anderson responds ironically.

At that moment, the court clerk approaches us, and says to me, 'There's someone on the telephone for you, Sir.'

I walk briskly to my office and pick up the phone.

'Hello, Judge Stephens speaking. Who's this?' I ask.

'You don't know me, Judge Stephens, but I have important information for you,' the muffled voice says.

'What is it?' I enquire.

'You *wazungu* are not welcome in our country. We will drive you out. All of you,' the voice insists.

'You can go to Hell first,' I say.

'No, Judge Stephens, it is you *wazungu* that will go to Hell first. *Ithaka na Wiyathi*!' The speaker answers emphatically.

'We'll see about that,' I reply, slamming the phone down.

'Black bastards and cowards,' I curse as my trembling hand knocks over the inkstand.

These *Mau Mau* are ruining the White Highlands but I'll do everything in my power to stop them. My mind travels back to my father's home in County

Kildare, as Colonel Stephens stood in front of his hearth with his jodhpurs and whip in hand telling me of his and his troops exploits in the Great War.

"We'd been in the trenches at Ypres for months on end with neither the Hun nor the Allies making any significant ground except at the expense of thousands of lives. My troops hadn't had a decent hot meal for weeks and their energies were sapped by the constant cold, mud, rain, vermin and nightly bombardments. They were very near to being completely dispirited and I said to them:

"When you're up against the enemy, and he thinks you've got nothing more to give and nowhere to go, you have to surprise him with your courage, audacity and determination. It's precisely these qualities that you need for victory. The harder they come at you, the stronger your resistance. That's what makes the British army almost invincible. We'll never be daunted. Remember that!"

Nevertheless, it was Edward's unshared and somewhat shameful memory that prevented him from entering the Military Academy at Sandhurst and following in his illustrious father's footsteps, Colonel Stephens. I can still feel the Chief Medical Officer's Report in my hands, crumpled from incessant perusal.

We regret that Mr Edward Stephens has not achieved the required standard in the recent Medical Examination due to a testicular hydrocele.

That crushing line brought to an end all my hopes of joining the Connaught Rangers Cavalry Regiment, the apogee of my boyhood ambitions. And what the devil difference will a "hydrocele" on my balls make, anyway? I mean for God's sake, does it prevent me riding a horse, shooting a weapon or leading men? I think and still feel.

To rub salt in this wound, I learned, subsequently, what my father's close friend had said about this incident.

'Ah, never mind, Robert, your son's tall and distinguished looking, and you can always put him in for the Bar.'

Before this calamity, I had never even considered a career in law. This painful recollection brings me back to the matter in hand.

Let's face it, these *Mau Mau* are a cowardly, barbarous and despicable bunch of savages who need to be taught a sound lesson. Nothing less than complete and utter elimination must be our goal.

The first thing I must do is evict these troublemakers from our province. That will settle their hash. If they resist, then we'll use all necessary and punitive force. It'll serve them right. The Robertsons' murder and the *Lari* Massacre are just the beginning of this rebellion, but they've underestimated our strength and resolve, and we won't be intimidated by their terror tactics, believe me.

I sit down at my desk, pick up my favourite fountain pen, and begin to write my "Action Plan" for cleansing the White Highlands of the *Mau Mau* scourge. The first words I write are: *Clear White Highlands of Mau Mau terrorists.*

Chapter Twelve
Munthu March 1953

I'm standing on the edge of my village, and know that if I ever go back to my *shamba,* the security forces will find me and arrest me and my family, and that I cannot risk. I start at some strange sounds believing that at any moment the *wazungu* security forces and their *askaris* will arrest me. It's early morning, and my kinsmen are outside their huts having food. As I stand here, not sure of which way to go, I see a neighbour, Jacob.

'*Hujambo,* Jacob, *habari ya maisha,* hello, Jacob, how's life?'

'*Sijambo,* Munthu, *maisha ningi mashauri,* we've a lot of problems.'

'*Gani, rafikiangu?* What's wrong, friend?'

'The security forces are throwing us off our *shambas* and forcing us to live in so-called "villages" and shacks surrounded by armed *wazungu na askaris.'*

'*Kwa nini?* Why?' I ask.

'They say that we are sending warriors from our tribe to join the *Mau Mau.'*

'But this is a lie. How can they believe this?' I ask him.

'*Rafikiangu,* they are punishing us for the *Mau Mau* struggle for *Ithaka na Wiyathi,* Land and Freedom.'

'*Ndio, kujua,* yes, I know.'

'*Vipi,* how?' He asks.

'I saw the security forces shoot innocent men, women and children from our tribe *kwa sokoni,* Nakuru market,' I reply.

'*Pole!* Sorry!'

'*Nimeshapoa,* thanks.'

'Now the *wazungu* will not stop until they have taken all our land and our families are starving,' I say.

'*Wana fanya nini,* what can we do?'

'*Sijui,* Jacob, I don't know, *lakini sasa na tuende mwitu,* but now I must go to the forest myself to escape the security forces.'

'*Kwa nini,* why?'

'General China, and his comrades forced me to be "look out" when they attacked and murdered our *wazungu* neighbours, the Robertsons, two moons ago.'

'*Ndio, rafikiangu,* yes, everyone in the village knows this now…'

'*Lakini, ni maisha ningi mashauri,* so I have my own troubles now, Jacob,' I say.

'*Salama* Munthu, *na safari nzuri,* go in peace, and have a safe journey.'

'*Salama* Jacob, *na kwaheri,* goodbye.'

After I bid Jacob farewell, I head for the Aberdare Forest.

Last time I left this dark forest, it was to see the Robertson family die at the hands of *Mau Mau.* Memories of that bloody time are carried in my veins, which sing out in atonement, like the sap of the *Inenge* tree. Where am I? These tracks I am trying to follow are so confusing. They are going in all directions, like a herd of wild buffalo. If I'm not careful, I'll end up back at General China's camp and will suffer for my mistakes.

I clench my stomach tightly as I remember those images of ragged, hungry faces staring at me from the forest clearing, dancing like unquenched flames in front of my eyes.

Am I not one of their tribe? Do I not share their blood? But they cannot ignore the prophecy. How can they believe they have more powerful *Gethathi,* magic than the *wazungu's* guns and armies?

As I think this, I trip and fall, smashing my head on the outstretched limb of an *Inenge* tree. 'Shit,' I wince as the jagged pain is followed by a coursing of warm blood over my forehead and into my perspiring right eyebrow, gathering in the corner of my mouth. As I dip my head instinctively, I notice a young man cowering to my left, sheltering under the spreading leaves of a giant bamboo.

'*Hujambo, kijana.*'

'*Sijambo, Kaka.*'

I can see he's trembling with fear, cold and hunger and his eyes study me cautiously. He is short, thin and dressed in what looks like a tattered servant's uniform.

'*Una fanya nini, kijana,* what are you doing here, young man?'

'I'm running, *Kaka.*'

'*Nani,* who from?'

'The security forces. '

'*Wapi kijana,* where are they?'

'*Karibu, Kaka*, very near, Uncle.'

'*Haraka! Ondoka!* Hurry! Let's go!'

'*Wenda wapi,* which way?'

We storm off into the forest like two startled gazelle, but I struggle to keep up with him and stop running. When I recover enough breath to start again, I see him still there, his skin glistening with perspiration as his body twists to avoid the thick forest vines all around us. His eyes seem to scan and penetrate the dense greens and browns of the canopy around us, like a stalking leopard. Suddenly, he stops and turns to me.

'*Kaka,* they'll not find us here. I hide here before.'

His chest heaves with deep breaths as he holds his bleeding cheek.

'*Pole,*' I console.

'*Nimeshapoa,* ' he responds.

We both wipe our wounds with the backs of our hands.

'*Gina laka, kijana,* what's your name?' I ask him.

'*Gina laka,* Bado, *Kaka.*'

'*Gina laka*, Munthu.'

'*Salamu*, Munthu.'

'*Salamu,* Bado.'

We smile and approach each other.

'Together we can escape,' I say.

'*Ndio kabisa, Kaka*, surely, Uncle.'

Before we can dwell on the beginnings of our desperate friendship, we both startle at the sound of gunshots.

'*Haraka. Ondoka*, Hurry! Let's go!'

Once again, we set out on the path which leads us further into the depths of the dark forest surrounding the Aberdare Mountains. We try to be quiet as we weave our way in and out of forest paths and vines. After a long time, cut, bruised and bleeding, we find ourselves in a clearing where a makeshift group of huts stand.

'*Hodi.* Anyone here?'

My words hang in the humid air.

Chapter Thirteen
Isabel Kingston Farm, 5 April 1953

If you look out across the expansive front lawn of Kingston Farm, which is surrounded by impenetrable forest to the north and east, and a steep decline of thorn bush and views across to the arid Rift Valley to the south and west, you will observe a huddle of familiar figures. Isabel is sitting with her bull mastiff, Cleo's head, on her thigh and she is grooming him carefully for ticks. Robert is asleep in his muslin-covered cot, and Rex, her Dachshund, is on the edge of the lawn thrashing his tail amidst the tangy smell of Hibiscus flowers, seeking out a terrified turtle.

As I carefully pluck the intransigent ticks out of Cleo's fur, I remember Ted's love of dogs, and the stories he told me about hunting to hounds in the Wicklow Mountains in his youth. He was "a real gent", a "West Brit", as my da used to say to me. But my first encounter with Ted was in Grafton Street, Dublin.

'Would you like to buy a bunch of primroses, Sir? It's for charity, only sixpence a bunch.'

There he was, tall, handsome and aristocratic, and smiling shyly at me out of his sky blue eyes. I knew it was "love at first sight". He told me he was studying for the Bar exams, and would I like to join him for one of his dinners at the Inns of Court. How romantic. And I was tempted. For that fleeting moment, I felt that Ted's love could carry me away to far off and exciting places where I would be happy and secure.

I certainly didn't want to end up like ma, married to a National School teacher with six children in tow. Yet here we are, in this God-forsaken outpost of Empire, living in fear of our lives. And now Robert's here, I can't even sleep for the worry of it all.

Mum would only say that I brought it upon myself. Then, when Ted and I fell out, and I went to stay with my cousin, Moira, in London last year, I met Francesco, the attaché to the Brazilian Ambassador. What a contrast he was to Ted—passionate, fluent and so incredibly sensuous. I had the feeling that he was a cultured man of the world, but married, alas! I remember our first meeting and what a handsome and dapper young man he was. I first met him at a party at the Brazilian Embassy in Belgravia.

My cousin, Moira, whom I was staying with in Knightsbridge at the time, asked me to go with her on this occasion. She introduced me to him.

'Senor Francesco, please let me introduce you to my first cousin, Isabel, from Dublin.'

'Senora Isabella, mi encanta, I'm delighted to make your acquaintance.'

From the start, I was attracted to this rather exotic man with his tall, elegant figure, sallow skin and charming manners. A man of the old school: chivalrous and somewhat romantic, I thought. When he spoke my name, "Isabella", with his inimitable Portuguese accent, I felt slightly weak at the knees, I must admit.

'Senor de Silva is the attaché to the Brazilian Ambassador,' Moira says.

'I'm pleased to meet you, Senor de Silva.'

'Perdon, Isabella, please call me Francesco.'

It was then that I noticed the twinkle in his eye.

'I like the way you pronounce my name, "Isabella" with your Portuguese accent.'

'Tell me, Isabella, how long are you staying in London?' He asks, deftly changing the subject.

'It depends how long it takes me to establish my modelling career.'

'Ah well, perhaps I can introduce to some of the attractive and interesting sights of London during your stay.'

'That would be lovely, Francesco,' I say, feeling flattered at his interest in me.

I didn't see Francesco until two weeks later. It was Easter Sunday, and he had invited me to Kensington Gardens to have a tour of the newly planted flower beds that spring. I was feeling buoyed up with anticipation, with the prospect of this charming man's companionship for the day, and I was dressed in one of my favourite outfits: a light blue blouse, pleated beige skirt and sensible walking shoes. I wore my loose auburn hair over my shoulders as it was a balmy spring day.

'Good morning, Isabella. Me encanta! How nice to see you again,' he greets me warmly.

'Good morning, Francesco. And how are you today?'

'I'm full of the joys of spring, as you say in English.'

'Likewise. Isn't it a fine spring day now?'

'It truly is. So where would you like to walk today, Isabella?'

'Shall we go and see the ducks on the pond first?'

'Of course, let's walk towards the palace and the pond,' Francesco says, taking my arm in his, a gesture which flatters me a little.

As we approach the large, circular pond, the south-easterly spring wind ruffles my hair, and I catch the distinctive smell of daffodils and apple blossom in the air. The sounds of the quacking ducks, pursuing each other with their mating rituals amuses me and Francesco as we exchange knowing smiles. Suddenly, a heron swoops in and leaves with a fish in its beak. Everyone watching the scene is somewhat taken aback.

Francesco comments, 'There you are then, Isabella. Amidst this idyllic spring calm, Nature shows she is red in tooth and claw.'

'You're right, Francesco, the cycle of life and death proceed under our very eyes, don't they?'

As we're standing there together by the pond facing Kensington Palace, I ask Francesco, 'Do you like living in London, Francesco?'

'I'm quite used to it by now, you know.'

'Where were you before London?'

'I was attaché to the ambassador of Brazil in Madrid.'

'What's Madrid like, Francesco?'

'You know, Isabella, Madrid is a beautiful city set up high on the meseta of Spain, overlooked by the mountains of Segovia.'

'I've never been to the Continent, Francesco, and I would so like to go one day.'

'I have a feeling you will go there one day, Isabella, perhaps with me?'

His question lingers in the air like the scent of apple blossom.

We continue walking around the huge pond opposite the palace, and I notice many families and courting couples enjoying their picnics with simple wicker baskets, tablecloths, plastic cups, saucers and plates neatly laid out.

And I think, fleetingly and a little guiltily, of Ted and me in St Stephen's Green in early March last year. Part of me feels as if I'm betraying his trust and another part of me still resents his possessiveness which began to repel me.

That's one of the many things I prefer about Francesco. He's such a positive and cultured man of the world. Sometimes I wish that Ted was more like him. Que sera sera. Whatever will be, will be, I sing to myself. Can a woman love two men?

'A penny for your thoughts, Isabella?'

I snap out of my momentary reverie and switch the pattern of my thoughts and speech.

'Ah...I was thinking about a book which describes bull-fighting in Spain.'

'Was it Hemingway's book, For Whom the Bell Tolls?'

'You're right, Francesco. It was him, and it was all about the Spanish Civil War, wasn't it?'

'That's it, Isabella. You have a good memory. What did you like most about Hemingway's book?'

'I liked his passionate descriptions of the ordinary Spanish people caught up in that terrible Civil War, and his veneration for comradeship.'

'Yes, that's it, Isabella. Hemingway's the consummate, yet terse, writer with a taste for the exotic and passionate in life.'

'I would love to travel and write, Francesco.'

'I have a feeling that you will travel, and perhaps live abroad one day.'

'Do you really think so, Francesco?'

'I really do.'

Suddenly, the south easterly wind picks up and the picnickers anxiously protect their precarious provisions, while a young boy cries out to his father at the fate of his upturned yacht in the pond. Francesco jerks me out of my preoccupations with his question.

'Do you think you will go back to Edward in Dublin?'

'I...I'm not sure, to be honest, Francesco. I've some hard thinking to do while I'm here in London.'

'It would be a shame to see you go, Isabella, and...'

'Well, at least I don't have to decide too soon, do I?' I interrupt clumsily.

As we stand facing the statue of King William and Queen Mary in front of Kensington Palace, I think to myself, yes, it's much too soon to decide to go back to Ted in Dublin. Life here seems far too exciting and interesting to do that and I think Ted and I need a cooling off period anyway. It'll do him good.

Towards the end of our pleasant excursion in Kensington Gardens, Francesco asks, 'Do you like opera, Isabella?'

'I adore it!' And I briefly recall Ted and me practising an aria from "La Boheme" together, when times were happier between us.

'Since you like opera so much, why don't I take you to Covent Garden one evening soon?'

'That would be lovely, Francesco,' I say, repressing my excitement at the prospect.

'Come on, Cleo. Keep still and stop whining. I know they're a devil to pull out. Be patient. I don't like it either you know.'

Cleo growls tolerantly and catches a locust in mid-flight, while Robert sleeps on in the cooler, late afternoon breeze of the frangipani-scented flower-borders.

With Ted, it's different. I've never felt truly accepted by him. He's always getting me to read books like *A thousand and one ways to improve your mind.* What's wrong with my mind anyway? Does it really make a heap of difference whether I know the reasons why the Roman Empire came to a sticky end, or how many miles it is to the sun?

Also I'm sick of those boring dinner parties and "blue stockings". They're only the wives of petty colonial officials, after all. More importantly, I know that Francesco accepts me for who I am. But now I find myself in darkest Africa without a friend, apart from Elena who has become a dear confidante to me.

Suddenly, Robert is awake and crying with hunger, so I get up and gather him into my arms for a feed, while an irritated Cleo and Rex scamper off into the forest to hunt.

Chapter Fourteen
Munthu

We look at each other with a mixture of fear and surprise as one by one, armed warriors emerge from their huts. It's too late to start running. And where could we run to?

I break the silence.

'We've lost our way, *wakaka*.'

The *Mau Mau* warriors begin laughing at us.

'*Ndio kabisa*, we can see that,' the tallest one cries out, grinning maliciously.

A warrior holding his spear at the ready asks, 'What brings you here, *wageni*?'

Thinking as quickly as my wits and trembling heart will allow, I reply, 'We're looking for General China, comrade.'

'*Saafi*. We can help you,' says the spear-carrier, grinning like a hyena and surveying his comrades. He turns to the warrior nearest him and says, 'Fetch boss.'

We huddle together for safety as the warrior enters a hut and then emerges with a familiar face, General China.

I try to conceal my fear as General China and his aide approach me and Bado.

'So you're back, comrade Munthu. I thought you had deserted us,' he says, grinning.

'You know I had to say *kwaheri* to my family, General China.'

'*Ndio kabisa*, surely. So now you're back. That's good!' General China says triumphantly.

His comrades laugh and cheer at his gentle irony.

'Who's this *kijana* with you, comrade?' General China asks.

'*Gina laka,* his name is Bado, General.'

'*Karibu kijana* and welcome to the honourable tribe of *Mau Mau*.'

'*Asante sana,* General,' Bado responds a little fearfully.

'We'll have to think of suitable job for you, Bado, in celebration of you joining us,' General China hints ominously.

'*Ndio,* General, I'll be honoured,' Bado replies, without irony.

I fidget uneasily at this suggestion.

'But before we do anything, I would like you to join us in a tribal ritual.'

'*Ndio kabisa,* yes, of course,' Bado and I chorus.

General China bends down and picks up a handful of mud which he smears on our faces in turn. As he does so, his comrades begin to chant the *Mau Mau Gethathi,* Oath, which ends, '*Ithaka na Wiyathi* will be ours when all *wazungu* are driven from our land.' We begin to mouth the words of this unfamiliar chant as we endure this "sacred marriage to the Earth" of our *Mau Mau* comrades. When the ceremony is over, we are led to the campfire and offered *posho* to eat and *pombe,* palm wine, to drink.

After we've been served with this simple fare, General China approaches us and says, 'I have a good job for you both.'

'*Gani,* what is it, General?' I enquire with feigned enthusiasm.

'You'll be our new *Wa-Gethathi,* Oath-takers,' General China responds.

'What will we have to do, General?' I ask, as if I didn't know.

'We'll send you to some villages in the forest and your job will be to persuade the young warriors to swear the oath, *Ithaka na Wiyathiau,*' he says.

For a brief moment, I felt as if our hearts had skipped a beat as I remember how the *Mau Mau* had "persuaded" many families to take the oath recently. I cover my hesitation with a beguiling smile, as does Bado.

'So when will we begin, General?' I ask hesitantly.

'As soon as you've rested from your journey, comrades.'

Bado and I look at each other with some foreboding as we both proceed to the hut allocated to us by the General.

Chapter Fifteen
Wa-Gethathi, Oath-Takers

The following morning, we wake with the dawn chorus of hungry birds chirping and chattering their beak-full progress as the sun's rays began to filter through the thick forest mist of the *Mau* escarpment. It rained heavily during the night, and grey clouds enshroud the mountain peaks. As I prepare *posho* for our breakfast over the glowing embers of the smoky fire, Bado asks me, 'What must we do to take *Gethathi*, oaths?'

'We will have to persuade the villagers that the *Mau Mau* oath is the only way that the villagers can protect their land from *wazungu*,' I reply.

'Have you seen how the oath-takers work and what happens to those who refuse it?' Bado asks.

'*Hapana*, no, but I've been told about their rituals,' I respond.

'I have also,' he says, and then he refers in great detail to what had happened to his unfortunate family some time ago.

When he's finished, I say, '*Pole, rafikiangu,* sorry, friend,' and grasp his shoulders in a comradely fashion, and we finish our *posho.*

'*Tuende,* let's get our orders from General China before he drives us out.'

'*Haya, tuende* yes, let's go,' Bado utters in agreement, as we get up to go.

We walk gingerly between the other warriors' huts until we arrive at General China's compound. He's already up and sharpening his *panga* with a whetstone, and eyes us with his hyena's grin.

'*Habari ako,* how are you?'

'*Salama tu,* well, General.'

'*Haya,* so this is where you are going and what you have to do.'

General China explains in detail to us the strategies of *Wa-Gethathi*, the oath-takers. He indicates, by drawing in the dirt, which villages the *Mau Mau* are targeting around the Aberdare Mountains and Mount Kenya, and how we should conduct the oath-taking ritual.

'Any questions, comrades?' General China says, as he concludes his briefing.

'What if the villagers refuse *Gethathi,* oath, General?' I ask.

The hyena smile re-appears on General China's pock-marked face:

'We kill them and burn their homes and *shambas,* of course!'

'*Ndio kabisa,* of course, General,' I respond, regretting my superfluous question.

'*Safari njema,* safe journey, comrades,' the General dismisses us both.

'*Salama tu,* peace to you, also,' we chorus as we proceed on our assignment.

Chapter Sixteen
Munthu and Bado An Isolated Village in the Heart of the Aberdare Mountains

A half-moon illuminates the small village hugging the mountain and trails of cooking fires can be seen drifting in a southerly direction as the damp, mantling mists begin clearing from the densely-wooded slopes of The Aberdare Range. The air has an eerie stillness that vibrates with our light footsteps as we follow the tortuous snaking of forest paths. Our only witnesses are the fruit-collecting macaque monkeys patrolling the canopy of trees and vines above us, and the omnipresent, rainbow-coloured canaries chirping zestfully.

'*Sissi hapa, sassa,* we're nearly there,' I whisper.

'*Kuona,* I can see *shambas*,' replies Bado.

'*Ku-kumbuka*, remember the plan?' I ask.

'*Ndio*,' responds Bado.

As we enter the village, we make our way quietly to the largest compound of huts, and call out: '*Hodi!* Who's there?'

There's no response, so we wait before repeating the greeting. At last, a young, statuesque warrior appears at the entrance to the compound.

'*Karibuni mgeni*, welcome!'

'*Habari asabuhi*, good morning,' we respond in unison.

'*Salama tu*, geetings to you, also.'

'I would like to speak to your chief about an important matter,' I say.

'*Kuja hapa, wageni*, come this way.'

Before we depart, we conceal our *pangas* in some bushes outside the compound.

The chief is tall, sinewy and has greying hair topped with a head dress that looks like a crushed *mzungu* hat. Immediately behind him, in the shadows of the hut, is one of his senior wives preparing cassava and coconuts for his breakfast.

'*Haya, wageni, una fanya nini,* hello, guests, what brings you here?'

'*Mzee,* we are here to help you rid our tribal lands of *wazungu,*' I say.

'*Vipi,* how?' The chief queries doubtfully.

'We are invoking the power of *Ngai,* and *Gethathi,* oaths against *wazungu,*' I say.

'Who sent you?' The chief asks suspiciously.

'General China, *mzee,*' I reply.

'*Kweli?*' The chief hesitates a moment and then adds, 'I'll call a meeting tonight, and see what we can do for you, *wageni.*'

'We are grateful to you, *mzee,*' I say, as we stand up to leave.

On the way to the guest hut, Bado and I observe the villagers at their daily routines. The women are going off with their daughters to collect water and firewood, and pounding maize meal, while the men sit around drinking *chai,* smoking, talking, or sharpening their *pangas* in small huddles, sitting on their haunches. Soon, an ornately dressed, senior wife of the chief greets us both.

'*Hodi! Wanapenda chakula, wageni,* would you like some food?'

'*Ndio kabisa, mama,* yes, please,' we respond enthusiastically.

The next moment, one of the village women comes in respectfully carrying a calabash of steaming *posho* and two bowls.

'*Asante sana, Mama,* thank you, mother,' we both intone in grateful unison.

'*Ku karibisha, wageni,* you are welcome!'

Between mouthfuls of *posho,* Bado asks me, 'Do you think they'll agree to *Gethathi,* oath-taking ceremonies tonight?'

'I'm not sure. The chief seems to know General China's reputation, so we may be in for a surprise,' I reply.

'I hope not,' says Bado shakily.

'*Wasiwasi,* don't worry. I'm sure it'll be favourable,' I reassure Bado, although my mind is full of doubts and fears.

I see much preparation and activity going on in the village that day. Goats are being herded into the chief's compound and elders from the surrounding villages have been invited to attend what looks like a land-marking ceremony. Groups of women in vivid *vitenge,* saris, pound maize meal, while the younger males gather great bunches of firewood and statuesque women carry overflowing gourds of *pombe,* into the chief's enclosure.

As *wageni,* guests, Bado and I are ushered into the company of the chief's clan, we are offered stools to sit on and pipe tobacco to smoke. We accept with gratitude. While some of the warriors present are greeting us, a large, tethered goat is ushered in and staked to the ground in the centre of the enclosure. A short, wizened shaman wearing ceremonial dress approaches the goat and examines it carefully. Once he's satisfied, he begins to prepare some herbs inside an open-ended gourd.

I turn to Bado and whisper, 'I hope the sacrifice of this goat will bring good fortune to our plan.'

'If God wills it,' Bado concurs.

Chapter Seventeen
Edward Nyeri Detention Centre, Rift Valley Province, 12 April 1953

There are lines of them, one after the other; their faces looking out at me with confusion, fear and hatred. Sometimes their faces are inscrutable, and at other times, they just look at me with something like contempt. Although, we have the power here, we have a questionable right to be sitting in judgement on them.

Yet among this seething Kikuyu rabble, there is someone guilty of the Robertsons' murder and they will pay the final price—if I can get my hands on them. Although, some misguided liberals talk about self-determination and independence for the colonies, like that damn fool Cameron, all I can see looking at these rows of ragged blacks, are ignorant peasants and idle, trouble-making *Mau Mau*, incapable of self-governance at any time.

I'm wearing my black judge's robes, which are flapping behind me as I stride across the compound being followed by a phalanx of armed *askaris*, and my Sikh Clerk of the court. I stop abruptly at the gate to Nyeri Detention Centre and dismiss my escort. As they return to the courthouse, I stare through the towering barbed wire fence, thinking.

'Judge Stephens,' a voice calls out to me in the middle distance.

'Who's that?' I reply.

'I think we have the blighters, Sir,' Anderson shouts.

'How do you know?' I respond, approaching him rapidly.

'We have informants, Sir,' Anderson replies.

'Let me see them,' I ask.

'Come this way,' Anderson replies.

I follow Anderson and the two *askari* down lines of black, haggard faces till we reach a small enclosure guarded by two armed policemen.

'Here they are,' Anderson says, pointing to two surly, bearded *Mau Mau*. The suspects are dressed in frayed blue overalls and tyre sandals fastened with lengths of badly-worn sisal threads. A smell of stale perspiration permeates the air around them.

As I look at these ragged, shifty men, they shuffle and shy away from my gaze. They certainly look capable of murder. I indicate to Anderson to follow me. We walk away from the barbed wire enclosure and stand as far down wind as we can.

'We'll need more than the evidence of your informants to try, convict and hang them,' I point out.

'Don't worry, Sir. We've searched their homes and found a blood-stained machete and a few personal effects belonging to the victims,' Anderson replies.

'Good. Well done, Mike. That's a really great start,' I say.

'Thanks, Ted,' he replies.

'They'll appear before me at nine o' clock tomorrow morning. Can you arrange that?' I ask.

'Of course, Your Lordship,' Anderson replies sardonically.

I'm glad to get away from that camp. The smell of urine, stale perspiration and worse was making me nauseous. At last, I've a way forward and we've caught the Robertsons' murderers. I ring Izzy from the court office in my excitement.

'Izzy, my darling. We've got the culprits,' I say enthusiastically.

'What culprits?'

'The Robertsons' murderers.'

'Really, Ted?' She asks.

'Absolutely. The informants and the reward led us to them,' I reply.

'What are you going to do now?' She asks.

'We'll try, and then we'll hang them,' I say.

The line goes quiet for a moment.

'Aren't you going to make martyrs of them if you do that, Ted?' She replies.

'What are you saying, Izzy? They murdered the Robertsons and now they'll hang for it,' I reply.

'Be careful, Ted. I believe there'll soon be others in their place,' Izzy says.

I don't know how to respond to this curious remark, so hold my counsel.

The next day, the colonial authorities begin the wholesale eviction of Kikuyu "squatters" and ordinary landed farmers in earnest, and over a million Kikuyu are forcibly removed from their farms and re-located into hundreds of fortified "villages" with watchtowers and trenches lined with deadly stakes. There are scenes of great brutality and mayhem as many refuse to move from their *shambas* and land they have lived on and farmed for generations.

The Kikuyu tribes mount fierce resistance in response, but their stones, spears, bows and arrows are no defence against the 303 rifles and sten guns of the British colonial police and army. Rioting and armed resistance to British rule spread like wildfire and soon the White Highlands is the scene of atrocity and counter atrocity as farms, dwellings and mission stations go up in flames.

Thousands of innocent Kikuyu are driven from their farms and interned without trial, and thousands more are interrogated, tortured, convicted and hanged. *Ithaka na Wiyathi*, Land and Freedom, becomes their rallying cry, and terrible suffering the price.

Within the first few weeks of the forced evictions and internments, *Gethatha,* oath-swearing ceremonies begin around campfires the length and breadth of the Rift Valley Province and elsewhere. The Kikuyu tribes gather in great numbers and swear the *Mau Mau Gethathi,* oath, *Ithaka na Wiyathi,* that there will be no rest until the last *mzungu*, Briton, has left their land and country. By the mid-1950s, ninety percent of the Kikuyu, Embu and Meru tribes have taken the oath and those who do not swear it are outcasts and their lives become forfeit.

Chapter Eighteen
Munthu and Bado

I'm standing next to Bado alongside the chief, and around us are young warriors testing each other for strength and skill in stick-fighting. The red ochre faces and white markings of the initiated warriors are blurring in front of my eyes as they out jump and outwit each other with their athletic movements and dances. Slowly, my attention is drawn away from the dancers to the loud invocations of the *Mondo Mogo*, shaman, who slits the throat of the tethered goat, catching its blood in a *calabash* which is then passed around the circle and all drink from it.

The *Mondo Mogo* calls everyone in the circle to silence and begins to incant a scared oath, raising his arms towards *Kere Nyaga,* the home of *Ngai*. He then takes the sharp knife proffered by his apprentice and slits the throat of the ram. It struggles courageously but is held firm by the young assistants. The *Mondo Mogo* then catches the first streams of the ram's blood in the *calabash*, and stirs in the herbs.

This concoction is then passed around the circle and all drink from it. The *Mondo Mogo* then removes the ram's stomach and proceeds to mark the designated land with its contents, while the elders of the tribe follow him in procession.

Behind the *wazee,* elders, come the young assistants, who plant trees and lilies (*matooka*) to denote the new boundary. While following the tail end of the warriors, Munthu whispers to Bado, 'We must make an announcement about the *Gethathi,* oath-taking, before the celebrations begin.'

When the elders and warriors are once more back in the circle of the compound, the chief gives a ewe to the *Mondo Mogo* as a token of gratitude for conducting the ceremony, and finally proposes a toast to the new land owner and his relative-in-law.

At this point, Munthu indicates to the chief his desire to speak. Before he does, the chief thanks the tribal elders in Gikuyu and asks Munthu to make his announcement.

'*Asante sana, mzee,*' says Munthu, shifting uneasily from foot to foot.

'*Wazee,* comrades, thank you for your trust and hospitality, and for allowing me to address you.'

Munthu feels the eyes and ears of his audience keenly in the pit of his stomach and he prays to *Ngai* that wise and convincing words will inspire his speech.

'Do you know that our lands are being taken from us by *wazungu* and the forces of the British Government?'

'*Ndio,* yes,' various warriors shout out.

'Are we going to let them do this to us?' I ask.

'*Hapana, hapana,* no, no.'

Heads began to shake and murmurs of dissent rise above the sound of the crackling fire and roasting ram.

'*Kweli,* we must resist them at all costs. These are our ancestral lands, the soul of our tribe, and they are robbing them from us.'

More raised assenting voices join in agreement. Munthu feels encouraged.

'How can we stop these thieves of our inheritance?'

As he pauses, voices chime in, 'Fight them,' they chant.

'*Ndio kabisa!* Yes, we'll fight them,' echoes Munthu, 'but first, we must use our powerful magic, our *Gethatha,* oath-taking ceremonies.'

At this point, Munthu looks over to the chief to gauge his reaction to his words, but the chief looks worryingly impassive. He continues, 'I propose we all now swear the *Mau Mau* oath, "*Ithaka na Wiyathi*", that "we will not rest until the last *mzungu* is driven from our ancestral lands".'

'*Ku-kubali.* do you agree?'

After some raised, assenting voices begin to quieten down, all eyes turn to the tribal chief who remains unnervingly still throughout Munthu's speech. The chief speaks, 'How can we resist the guns and armies of the *wazungu*? Are our *Gethathi,* oaths, enough?'

Chapter Nineteen
Isabel Kingston Farm, 5 May 1953

Already the heat of the morning African sun is driving the buffalo herds in search of water on the arid plateau, and among the groups of distant zebra and wildebeest grazing on the edge of the Rift Valley before it drops seven thousand feet to the parched Athi plain below, you can make out the dust of a moving vehicle. Isabel is watching the vehicle's approach through her field glasses and with mounting anticipation, as she has been expecting a letter from Francesco these last few days. She runs downstairs and calls for her servant.

'Juma, *Kuja hapa,* come here.'

'*Ndio, Memsab.*'

'*Posta kuja.* Please collect the letters for me.'

'*Ndio, Memsab.*'

Juma leaves by the front door and makes his way rapidly to the guarded farm entrance. Soon, the post Land Rover arrives. Juma collects the pile of letters and gives them to Isabel.

'*Asante sana*, Juma.'

'*Hata kidogo, Memsab.*'

Isabel walks slowly upstairs going through the letters to find Francesco's unmistakable hand. Here it is, thank God. Isabel holds it to her bosom and enters her room. Going to her dressing table, she picks up the paperknife and proceeds to open Francesco's letter. She lies down on the marital bed to read her lover's long-awaited words.

5 April 1953

From the Attaché to the Brazilian Ambassador
Snr. Don Francesco do Nascimento
3 Kensington Place

My darling Isabella,

I haven't been the same since the day we parted after our last night at the "Leopard's Club" in Soho. I still remember that glorious night of romance and passion with a warm glow. I've not met your equal in a Tango dancer, my love. You were made for it. Your brief time with me in London has many happy memories for me still.

Isabel looks out through her Bougainvillaea-framed window to the savannah beyond and takes a deep and longing draught of air into her lungs before she resumes the letter.

You have many admirers in my circle, Isabella, and if things don't work out with you and Ted in your little town in Africa, you know you are most welcome here at any time. To be honest, I've missed you terribly.

And I've missed you terribly, too, Francesco, Isabel responds in thought and feeling.

How are things between you and Ted? Does he still browbeat you with his superiority and high culture? Admit it, you and he are not compatible. I've rarely met such a proud and arrogant man. I assume all Anglo-Irish behave like that?

It wasn't always like that, Isabel reflects sadly. I remember my first night out with Ted, while he was at the Inns of Court in Dublin completing his Bar exams, and having to persuade him to dine at Switzer's Restaurant. He said it was far too expensive and pretentious. Francesco is so Latin and generous in comparison. She resumes.

You and I, on the other hand, are on the same wavelength, aren't we? We're ordinary mortals with artists' souls and a passion for life. I wish you had stayed in London and taken up your RADA place or continued with your modelling career. What a waste! Your life would have been very different here with me if you hadn't got engaged and married to Ted. Ce'st la vie!

You've no idea, have you, why I got married to Ted. Of course I loved you and enjoyed your lively, passionate, romantic company. But it couldn't carry on like that. After all, you were married already, and I had to think of my own future for a change. I had no future with you in London, really, did I?

The truth is, Francesco, I had very little choice and I hope to tell you why some day. But I had no option but to marry Ted and get on with my life as best I could. God, how I wish it had been different. I read on.

Do let me know how it's all working out? I miss your embraces and kisses so much, my darling. Write soon, my love, and tell me all your news. Know that you are always in my heart and mind, and that I truly adore you.
Your ever devoted,
Francesco
Attaché to the Brazilian Ambassador.

My God, why do I still feel such passion for Francesco? I can't get him out from under my skin. And yet I can't let my love for him overcome my loyalty and compassion towards Ted. I must tell him to stop writing. This pretence and subterfuge are draining me.

I replace the carefully folded letter in the envelope and slide it under my pillow with the intention of reading it again later. Elena is calling for me, so I leave the bedroom quickly.

Chapter Twenty
Munthu and Bado
Are *Gethathi*, Oaths, Enough?

Everyone's eyes turn towards the chief who looks around his clan with impassive eyes. There is silence, apart from the sounds of the crackling fire, cooking meat and the singing of countless tree frogs and cicadas. I answer the chief's question.

'*Mzee,* the future of your clan and of all our people depends on the successful outcome of this struggle for *Ithaka na Wiyathi.*'

The chief responds, slightly expanding his chest, '*Vipi,* how can we defeat the *wazungu* armies with our *Gethathi,* oath-taking, spears, bows and arrows?'

'*Ngai* will protect us, *mzee,* and give us justice. We can also withdraw our labour from the *wazungu.* After all, they cannot cultivate their tea, coffee and sisal without our help, can they?' I reply rhetorically.

At this response, the chief smiles wryly and raises his arms to quell the growing chorus of murmurs. He speaks, 'So, my people, what do you say to *mgeni's* opinion that we should swear the *Mau Mau Gethatha, Ithaka na Wiyathi?*'

There is a subdued murmur of assenting voices but the *mondu mogo* is the first to respond to his chief's question.

'*Mzee, Mothongo ne athogonjire borori,* the white man has spoiled and disgraced our country. I believe we have no choice except to swear the *Mau Mau Gethathi.* The power of *Ngai na mababu,* our ancestral spirits demand *Ithaka na Wiyathi,* Land and Freedom.'

Bado and I are so relieved and we slowly survey the group of assembled warriors and *wazee,* elders with expectation. One by one, they raise their right arm and shout their agreement with the *mondu mogo.*

'*Patana, patana,* we agree, we agree.'

The die is cast. When the assenting voices quieten down, the chief's voice booms aloud.

'*Ku-patana*, so be it. Prepare yourselves for *Gethathi*, oath-taking ceremony.' He turns to me and says, 'What are you waiting for?'

I approach the *mondu mogo* and say in a respectful tone, 'Can you make a sacrificial offering to *Ngai* to sanctify the oath-taking ceremony?'

'*Ndio, mgeni*, I will prepare a *calabash* of blood and herbs from a goat,' he replies and promptly summons one of his assistants who goes off in search of a suitable sacrifice.

In the meantime, I consult with the chief as to the form of the *Gethathi*, oath-taking ceremony, while another apprentice and the *mondu mogo* begin to prepare an ochre and chalk paste, *ira*, with which to anoint the oath-takers.

Eventually, the *mondu mogo's* assistant returns with a young goat and gives it into the care of his master. The chief quietens the feasting assembly and instructs one of his senior warriors to strike out a ceremonial rhythm on his *ngoma*, drum. Gradually, the assembled warriors form themselves into a circle and begin a circular dance, pounding their feet rhythmically in time to the beats of the *ngoma*. After some time, the *mondu mogo* halts the dance, comes into the centre of the circle of warriors and raises both arms towards *Kere Nyaga*.

As he does so, be begins to intone the sacred words of the offering, '*Thathaya Ngai!* May we be free of the blight of the *wazungu*,' and taking the ritual knife from his assistant, he slits the throat of the young goat. As he does so, he catches the first gouts of blood in his *calabash* which he mixes with sacred herbs. The ritual *calabash* is then passed around the circle of warriors and elders, which each of them sips before I administer the *Mau Mau Gethathi* with the help of the *mondu mogo* and his apprentice.

I thank my ancestors for the wisdom to help me keep calm throughout the ritual. When all the warriors and elders of the chief's tribe have sworn the *Mau Mau Gethathi*, he turns to them and says, '*Asante sana, wageni.* Your work is now done. Please give my *salamu* to General China. *Safari njema,* safe journey.'

'*Salama mzee,* peace be with you, Sir,' Bado and I reply in unison, as we bid the chief's clan farewell.

As we walk out of the forest clearing, and along the forest paths we first entered the village the day before, the sounds of the rhythmic *ngoma* and tribal dances begin to recede, while the chorus of tree frogs and cicadas gain the ascendancy.

Chapter Twenty-One
Tuende Nyumbani, Homeward

After some time, we reach the forested summit of one of the Aberdare Mountains, and are breathless and perspiring heavily. We've been following winding buffalo and human tracks and frequently have to stop and hack our way through proliferating lianas and bamboo. The forest mist has become virtually impenetrable and we lose our way several times. I signal to Bado to stop.

'*Ku-pumzica sasa, rafikiangu,* let's rest here a moment,' I say, as I wipe the perspiration from my brow with the back of my arm.

'*Mimi ku-choka*, I'm also tired,' Bado nods, and mimics my gesture.

'*Wata fanya nini*, what shall we do now?' Bado asks me.

'*Si-jui*, I'm not sure,' I reply.

'I can't face returning to General China's village,' I say hesitantly.

'*Kwa nini*, why not?' Bado asks.

'*Lakini*, because I want to return home to my family,' I reply. 'Also I don't trust General China.'

'*Kweli*, really?' Bado asks.

'*Kweli*, he is just using us. Once he has no further use of us, I'm sure we'll be killed.'

'*Nataka tuende, mimi na wewe*, can I come with you, Munthu?' Bado asks.

'*Ndio*, but you realise that General China will kill us if he discovers we've deserted *Mau Mau*?'

'*Ndio kabisa*, yes, that's right,' Bado responds mutedly.

'*Tuende, rafikiangu*, let's go then, friend,' I urge.

As we set off down the slopes of the Aberdare Mountains, there is lightness in the spring of our step as the dread of more oathings, killings and burnings recede with the dispersing damp mists and the welcoming warmth of the sun's rays. Soon we are into walking rhythm, and Bado asks, 'Do you really believe we can overcome these *wazungu*?'

'*Si jui,* I don't know, but I think *mababu*, our ancestors, are asking us to fight for justice,' I reply.

'*Ndio kabisa,* I agree entirely,' Bado responds.

There follows a silence between us as I begin to reflect on the tortuous journey that has led me to Bado, beginning with the prophecy and the violent destruction of my kinsmen by the security forces in Nakuru market, meeting General China and witnessing the murder of the Robertson family, and my fateful role.

I have a feeling that I'm being led reluctantly on a path that is taking me further and further away from those I love: Wambui, Eliza and Sam. They are precious to me, and I hate the fact that I'm now caught between the *Mau Mau*, on the one hand and the vengeful security forces on the other. My initiation into the age grade of my tribe has taught me one important lesson: that life has to be endured with courage and determination, and I resolve to be true to this sacred truth.

Chapter Twenty-Two
Family Reunion

As Bado and I crest the last undulating ridge, I can see ahead of us the warming and familiar sight of my father-in-law's village. It's laid out before us like a winding, sisal rope with collections of homesteads on the fraying edges. The smoke of cooking fires and the sounds of children laughing and playing brings a surge of hope and almost tears to my eyes. And I thank God that they have not been forcibly evicted by the security forces.

'*Sasa kufika,* we've arrived!' I shout with delight.

Bado smiles broadly and grasps my arm.

'*Tuende,* let's go,' I say as we both set off down the slope to my village and homestead.

As we approach the outlying homesteads, a gathering of uninitiated boys begin to circle round us like honey bees. Something deep inside me resonates with the thought that I'm beginning to honour the wisdom and courage of my manhood in this unequal struggle with the *wazungu,* the appearance of which my ancestors and elders had jokingly equated with the *kiengere,* a small light-coloured frog! These interlopers and despoilers of our ancestral lands would not be satisfied until they had occupied every *shamba* and termite nest.

I now know that it is my sacred duty to prevent this tragedy, with or without the help of the *Mau Mau.* I have to create a solid future for my wife and family on our sacred land.

Following the tortuous interlacing of footpaths, we arrive at our *shamba,* our ancestral land. All around us there is growing an abundance of *mahindi, maharagwe na mihogo,* maize, beans and, cassava, which kindle feelings of pride and warmth in my wife's conscientious labours. Suddenly, a joyous voice rings out, which has Wambui's unmistakable timbre.

'*Karibuni mume,* welcome, husband! *Karibuni mgeni,* welcome, friend!'

I can no longer restrain myself and I sweep Wambui off her feet and hold her close for a few precious seconds. Regaining my composure, I introduce my friend, Bado.

'Wambui, *mimi rafikiangu*, this is my friend, Bado.'

'*Karibu sana,* you are very welcome, Bado. *Safari njema*, how was your journey?'

Wambui welcomes Bado warmly, shaking his outstretched hand in both of her own.

'*Safari ndefu,* long, *Mama,*' Bado replies with a broad smile.

'*Njoo watoto*, come, children!' Wambui beckons our children.

As if by instinct, Sam and Eliza appear, running down the path to meet me. Eliza, being the tallest, reaches me first and throws herself into my outstretched arms.

'*Baba, Baba,*' is all that she can say, hardly restraining her tears of joy at seeing me again. Sam follows seconds later, launching himself at me with outstretched arms.

'*Iko wapi, iko wapi, Baba,* where have you been?' Sam says, as if I had just been on a short trip.

'I've been to the Aberdare Forest and had lots of adventures, which I will tell you about. *Huyu, rafikiangu,* here's my friend, Bado,' I add.

'*Karibu sana,* you are very welcome, Bado,' Eliza and Sam chorus.

Bado smiles his warmest smile and shakes hands with them both.

'*Tuende,* let's go,' Wambui says, and motions the party towards our dwelling.

I walk up the path to my wife's hut, escorted by my beloved children who are proudly acknowledging me to their playmates who circle around the pair of us with jests and cries of delight.

'How long are you staying, *Baba*?' Eliza asks.

'I can only stay a short while, Eliza. The security forces are still looking for me,' I reply mutedly. Eliza's hand presses mine more firmly as she looks up at me.

At the same time, Sam pulls at my right arm and says, '*Baba,* I can't wait to show you what I've been making!'

'I look forward to that, *mwanangu,* my son, *ndio kabisa,* very much!' I reply.

As we reach Wambui's dwelling, a party of village wives has gathered outside her hut, awaiting instructions for the preparation of a welcoming feast. After greeting and thanking them all, Wambui whispers something in my ear, and I lower myself to speak to Sam.

'*Tuende mwanangu,* let's go, my son, and choose a goat for tonight's sacrificial feast.' I beckon to Bado and the three of us go off to the livestock enclosure.

Warmth kindles in Wambui's anxious heart as she watches the men and boy walk away up the path to the *boma,* as straying chickens weave in and out. Maybe there is a future for us, after all? She reflects and prays to her spirit ancestors, *mababu na Ngai.* Perhaps we will all find safety and protection in the troubled times ahead.

Chapter Twenty-Three
Sam The Arrest of Munthu and Bado

'Hey. I've got an idea. Let's make a bow. First, find the right wood. Something flexible, like for hoop-making. Cut it to a man's height, then strip and steam it in a gourd. Out of this, I can create a bow so I can then have target practice with my friends. I'll make the best one I know.'

While I'm stripping my acacia branch, I can see my sister, Eliza, eyeing me with jealousy. I must remember to hide it when I've finished, or she will steal it from me, like that hoop I really liked. Another nick here and push it...hard. Yes, it's going into place nicely, but what's happening over there.

There are angry shouts and curses. A group of *wazungu* soldiers with guns is leading my father and Bado up the path. They look very frightened. I shout, '*Mama, haraka,* Mother, hurry! *Baba, una fanya nini*? Father, tell me what's happening?'

'*Ku-nyamaa,* Sam. Quiet or you will be punished. *Wenda,* go!' *Baba* shouts to me.

'*Hapana, Baba*! No, I'm not going! *Ku-toka wazungu*! Leave him,' I cry out as I see the soldiers dragging my father away. They push, shout, hit and curse him. They call him *Mau Mau* scum. I hate them. I want to kill them all.

'*Ku-simama*!' I scream at the top of my voice. '*Ku-simama*! Stop!'

I throw myself at their legs like a wild boar. Women of my tribe wrestle me to the floor as I scream and howl like a captured beast. I run off to find mama. Perhaps she can stop them?

Wambui

'*Mama, Mama,* the *wazungu* have taken *Baba*! Stop them! I beg you!' He shouts, and entwines himself around me desperately.

'*Ndio,* yes, *Mama*. Please help *Baba*! *Tafadhali!*' Eliza echoes.

Eliza and Sam scream loudly into my ears. I hug the children close to me as they cry desperately for me to save *Baba*. But I'm defenceless in the face of these relentless *wazungu* with their ruthless *askari* and guns.

'*Wasiwasi*, don't worry, we shall see *Baba* again. *Ahadi*, I promise.'

Even as I say these words, I feel how hollow they are. I can only pray to our ancestor spirits for justice. For a brief moment, I had hoped that Munthu and I could have enjoyed some freedom and peace, but it was not to be. When he left me and the children after he was forced to join the *Mau Mau*, I knew in my heart that he would always be a fugitive. I curse the *Mau Mau* for forcing him to take the hateful *Gethathi,* oath.

All we wanted was a quiet and peaceful life with our beloved *watoto*, tending to our *shamba*. I remember the day we agreed to buy our land. We paid ten goats and two cows for it, and it was so fertile. I could grow all that we needed in *mahindi, maharagwe na mboga*, maize, beans and vegetables. Our hut was built with the help of our clan and it overlooked the valley of our ancestors, who continued to bless us until today.

These *wazungu* have no respect for us at all. *Mothongo ne athogonjire borori*, the white man has despoiled and disgraced our country. And now they have taken my beloved Munthu from me. *Ngai na mababu wa-tukana wazungu,* may God and our ancestors curse these British for all time.

Munthu

When I awake that morning after the welcome feast, all I can hear is the tuneful chirping of birds and the sounds of mothers and daughters starting fires and trekking to the river for water. As for my beloved Wambui, she is already up and preparing *posho na mahogo* for our morning breakfast. As I lie here, I'm thinking, *Wapi,* where is Sam?

Then, I hear urgent voices and angry shouts. I rise quickly to investigate, but before I'm fully dressed, an *mzungu* police officer with his escort of armed *askaris* is at the hut's entrance.

'Is your name Munthu Mkesi?' The officer demands.

'*Ndio*,' I reply.

'Then come with us.'

'What do you want from me, *Bwana*?' I ask.

'You are being arrested on suspicion of being a member of the *Mau Mau* terrorist organisation.'

I feel suddenly weak and sickened in my stomach, but I breathe deeply and try to control myself.

'*Hapana,* no, *Bwana*. I've been staying here with my family for months. Ask my wife.'

'That's no concern of ours, boy. Come now, Mkesi, or it will be worse for you.'

'*Bwana,* please *tafadhali,* I can't leave my wife and children.'

'*Mau Mau* scum,' he says and strikes me in the face with his revolver, and then the *askaris* beat me to the ground with their rifles.

Sam comes to my aid and I tell him to be quiet and go away. He's a very brave boy and fights for my freedom. I cannot remember more.

Chapter Twenty-Four
Journey to Hola *Mau Mau* Scum!

The *askari* shouts at me as he hits me in the face with his rifle butt. I fall back against the canvas side of the *gari*, jeep, and feel the blood flowing down my cheek and under my collar, soaking my shirt. The searing pain turns into a constant throbbing as I try to hold my head in my hands. I realise I can't as they have handcuffed my hands to the wheel arch of the *gari*.

Bado and I are both slumped like sacks of cow dung in the back of the *gari* as it bounces along the rutted, dusty tracks towards an uncertain destination. I squint through the drying blood in my eyes and can see Bado looking sadly at the sight of the shrinking village, and resembling *simba,* lion's prey. Knowing that I can't reach out and reassure Bado, I turn my attention inwards and am met with the sad image of Wambui, Eliza and Sam huddled together by our hut with tears streaming down their faces.

The journey in this infernal *gari* seems endless. The blood in my scalp and face is encrusted, and the pain reminds me of my initiation ceremony all those years ago. I know I can endure this suffering but I have to ask myself, to what purpose? They have refused us water and food the whole time of our journey, and I'm worried about Bado, as he has hardly stirred from his iron bench seat, and I can see that the handcuffs have cut deep into his wrists because of the way he has been laying. Is he dead?

Before I can discover the truth of my question, I can see we are approaching a military camp or prison. I smell it. The wind carries it. There are high towers with men carrying guns in them. Everywhere there is sharp wire and row upon row of grey tents and some wooden huts. Now I can see many hundreds of my tribe staring hopelessly through lines of razor wire fences. They are like cattle waiting to be slaughtered, and I wonder what will happen to Bado and me.

'Get out, you *Mau Mau* scum!' The *wazungu* officer shouts as his *askaris* beat Bado and I out of the *gari* with rifle butts. Bado lies in a heap while they carry on beating him.

'*Ku-simama, Bwana; ku-simama, Bwana,* stop! I beg you,' I shout.

They start doing the same to me and I pass out. The next thing I remember is lying in a dark, evil-smelling cell, and it's unbearably hot and airless. My throat is dry as ash, and I am sick and aching from the beatings. Every bone in my head and body feels broken and I feel as if *Ngai* has abandoned me.

As I'm lying on the stinking floor of my solitary cell, I can hear a low humming as though the earth is speaking to me. Strangely, it reminds me of a distant time when I found myself in a forest clearing, skirting the edges of *Kere Nyaga*, where I had ventured as a boy on many occasions against my parents' wishes.

How real nature around me had seemed then, the parched grasses, the stunted evergreens, giant lobelias, and the peaty, spongy soil under my feet. Everything seemed to possess a living, vital energy that moved with a pulsating light and gentle vibration. My body was suffused with the Life Spirit and swayed gently with its rhythms. I feel comforted and safe, so I retreat to this place in my mind.

The green slopes around *Kere Nyaga* seem to undulate like a slow-moving *nyoka*, snake, upwards into the frozen white necklace encircling *Ngai*. I feel the earth I'm standing on move around the brilliant pole of the sun while my ears are filled with the low purring of a satiated *simba,* lion. And then the voices of my spirit ancestors begin to speak to me as I listen deeply in the stillness.

'*My son, you have heard us and you remember that we called you in to being before time. You chose this path of suffering because only through suffering does the spirit grow in knowledge and wisdom. You are a short while on this earth, and you have much to accomplish through understanding and accepting the workings of fate. Although, you have lost those you love most, we are still watching over you, and are proud of what you have achieved in your short life.*

'*We want you to know that the struggle for justice you are engaged in is a crucial one, and that your part in it is difficult and heroic. Know that one day, sooner than you believe, you will be united with all your family and the lands of your ancestors will be saved and protected from those to whom it does not belong. Continue on your journey knowing that we are with you each step of your path, listen to us, make offerings, and above all, have courage and faith always in the difficult times ahead. Salaam mwanangu, peace be with you, my son.'*

As I listen to these comforting words, something within me feels consoled and healed. I now know without doubt that my life has a purpose, and I feel reassured that I will eventually see my family again, despite the fact that images of Wambui, Eliza and Sam are never far from my mind. I'm also afraid for Bado, as I've not seen him since we arrived in this dark hell-hole of a prison.

Chapter Twenty-Five
Ku-kumbwa, Interrogation

I find myself in a cramped cell with my arms handcuffed behind my back balanced on a wooden chair. Opposite me is a stocky *mzungu* bulging out of his khaki uniform with a leather truncheon in his belt. My vision is blurred because I can hardly see out of my badly swollen eyes. There is blood in my mouth and I have lost some teeth. I'm afraid to lift my gaze in case these *wazungu* guards decide to beat me some more.

'So, boy, what happened to your *kipande*?' The officer asks.

'I lost it, *Bwana*,' I answer.

'You know it's illegal to be without it?'

'Yes, *Bwana*.'

'So where were you living before we found you in Nakuru?'

'My home is in Nakuru, *Bwana*.'

The officer slaps me hard around the face, and I can barely hold on to the table.

'I didn't ask you where your home is, boy, I asked you where you were living.'

'I was cultivating my *shamba*, *Bwana*.'

'So why did you leave your *shamba*, boy?' The officer shouts.

'I was running away from *Mau Mau*, *Bwana*.'

The officer takes his truncheon from his belt and smashes it into my head. I fall on the floor and the officer kicks me many times. I can't breathe and my groin is *ku-kumbwa*, stinging badly.

'You mean you were running to find your *Mau Mau* scum, weren't you!'

'*Hapana*, no, *Bwana*!'

'So why did you leave, boy?'

'The *Mau Mau* was burning villages, *Bwana*.'

'You stinking liar!'

The officer kicks me some more.

'You and your *Mau Mau* scum murdered the Robertson family, didn't you? Admit it, before I break every bone in your body!'

'*Hapana,* no, *Bwana*!'

I don't remember what happened after that. I wake up in my dark, stinking cell feeling I have been trampled by a herd of elephants, *ningi ku-kumbwa,* and it stings a lot. In the corner of my cell, there are some curling crusts of bread and a chipped tin mug of water. I feel sick and I wonder if I will ever get out alive and see my family again. I'm not sure what day it is or how long I've been here.

I'm only aware of the sound of slamming iron doors and muffled cries and screams. My mouth is dry like ashes, every bone and muscle aches, *ningi ku-kumbwa,* and my stomach is gripped by hunger.

While I am trying to bring the memories of Wambui, Eliza and Sam to my mind and imagine us all together again, I can hear the sound of army boots marching towards my cell, and I dread what is in store for me. The key turns in the lock and *wazungu* voices bark orders at me, 'Get off the floor, boy, and come with us!'

As I struggle to my feet, two *askari* with rifles handcuff my hands behind my back. The *mzungu* officer pushes me out my cell and curses under his breath, 'Stinking *Mau Mau* scum.'

I find myself back inside my *ku-kumbwa,* torture room, but this time there is a typed sheet of paper on the desk and a pen. I look at the *mzungu* officer who tells me, 'It's your confession to the murder of the Robertson family.' He goes on, 'You have two choices, boy.'

'What, *Bwana*?'

'Either you sign this confession now or we take you outside the camp and shoot you for trying to escape.'

'I see, *Bwana*.'

'You'd better see, boy.'

I realise I have no choice here, and sit down in front of the desk, while one of the *askari* takes my handcuffs off so I can sign my "confession to murder". As I sign my name, slowly and painfully, I wonder if my fate also has been written. The *mzungu* officer smiles a false, satisfied smile, and orders the *askari* to handcuff me again.

'You did a wise thing, *Mau Mau* scum. We'll see you before the judge.'

After that, I am pushed out of the room and escorted back to my cell by the *askari* who gives me a parting kick. At least I avoided further torture *na ku-kumbwa*, I feel with relief. And now I await my fate.

Chapter Twenty-Six
Edward Betrayal Kingston Farm,
5 May 1953

I return to Kingston Farm earlier than normal in order to collect some vital papers for the murder trial the next day. Izzy isn't at home, so she must have gone to the market in Kitale with Elena to purchase some fresh fruit and vegetables. I go upstairs to our bedroom, which is where I left the trial papers before I went to sleep the previous night. I can't find them on the floor by the bed, so I look under both the pillows and find a letter.

Do I recognise this hand? Yes. It's a letter from Snr Don Francesco de Nascimiento, Izzy's witness at our wedding. I carefully remove the letter from the envelope and read it, stopping from time to time to re-read it, paragraph by paragraph.

It's incredible! How could I have been such a trusting dupe? I can't believe that I fell for her cock and bull story about her visit to a London fashion agent in the first place. She deliberately set out to deceive me from the very start. Damn her! Damn her! Damn her! What a deceiving bitch!

I begin to beat Isabel's side of the bed with my riding whip bursting with grief and rage. 'Take this, and that! This and that!'

I continue exacting vengeance on the marital bed until I'm spent and sprawled on top of it. I doze into sleep with exhaustion and drift into the memories of my first meeting with Izzy's parents, Patrick and Eileen, whom I met in a leafy suburb of Dublin in the late summer of 1950.

Knock, knock.

'Hello, do come in, Mr Stephens. We've been expecting you,' says Eileen, opening the door to me.

I'm standing in the red doorway of Charleston Avenue with a winning smile and wearing a light-coloured raincoat, suit and my favourite yellow cravat.

'Ah, good evening, Mrs Haines. I'm delighted to meet you,' I say politely as I cross the threshold and remove my summer raincoat.

'Do come through to the drawing room, Mr Stephens, where we've been expecting you.'

'It's a pleasure to make your acquaintance, Mr Stephens,' says Patrick.

'Do take a seat by the piano,' he adds, indicating the settee where Izzy has been sitting and waiting for me to arrive. She comes to my side and we kiss in a genteel manner. Taking my proffered hand, she sits down alongside me.

'Can I get you something to drink, Edward?' Patrick asks.

'A dry sherry would be delightful, thank you, Mr Haines,' I say.

'Do call me Pat, Ted, if that's all right with you.'

'I shall, Pat, thanks, and do call me Ted.'

Pat goes over to the drinks cabinet and pours himself and me a sherry. As he does so, he calls out to Eileen who is in the kitchen putting the finishing touches to the Sunday roast.

'Will you be having a sherry too, Eileen?'

'I will now,' Eileen calls back.

Pat pours another glass for his wife and as he does so, he asks Isabel: 'And, Izzy darling, what'll you be having now?'

'I'll have a dry sherry, too, Da, thanks,' she replies.

'Well, Izzy, this is a little adventurous for you now, isn't it? It's usually a lemonade you'll be drinking, isn't that so?' Pat says teasingly.

'Ah, come on, Da. Don't cod me in front of Ted, will you now?' Isabel says with a cheeky smile.

'All right, my darling, I promise not to embarrass you in front of your beau.'

'Thanks, Da.'

When the three of us are sitting comfortably, Pat opens the pre-dinner discussion with what he believes to be a safe topic: music.

'So Ted, Izzy tells me you have a flair for music. Is that so?'

'I do indeed, Pat. I'm terribly fond of opera and the Irish ballads in particular.'

'And which ones do you like most of all?'

'Well, I'm very fond of singing "Danny Boy", "Carolan's Air" and "Down the Sally Gardens".'

I could see from Pat's expression that there was an immediate warming to me, the "West Brit" that Izzy, her eldest daughter, had brought home for the first time.

'Ah, now that's grand, Ted. And do you know who wrote the libretto for "Down the Sally Gardens", Ted?'

'Well, to be honest with you, Pat, I don't really know.'

'He's our greatest living treasure.'

'You don't mean W B Yeats, do you by any chance?'

'I do indeed, Ted, and I admire your taste in music and poetry, at least,' Pat says with a wry smile.

'And Ted's got a lovely singing voice,' Izzy chips in.

'Now, is that a fact?' Pat responds, beaming at his daughter.

'Izzy has a perfect soprano voice, too, Pat. And I sense that she comes from very musical stock. Isn't that so?'

''Tis indeed, and perhaps after dinner, we can have a session around the piano here,' Pat says, warming to the musical theme.

'And did you know that da's a great fiddle player, Ted?'

'You and your family are truly full of musical talent, aren't you,' I say.

'Well, Izzy, I think you've chosen something of a musical romantic here in Ted, haven't you?'

Izzy blushes at this comment, and excuses herself in order to help her mother with dinner. When Isabel is in the kitchen and out of earshot, Patrick poses the question that has preoccupied him for the last three months.

'So, Ted, now we have the floor to ourselves, can you tell me what your intentions might be regarding my dear Izzy?'

I shift a little uneasily in my seat and gather myself for a considered response.

'I'm so glad that we can speak openly about the matter now, Pat, and I will say unambiguously that Izzy has won my heart and I expect that I shall be knocking on your door quite soon to seek your daughter's hand.'

Pat can't quite contain his surprise and joy at this unexpected utterance and says, 'Let me be clear, Ted. When you do honour your intentions, you will be taking the apple of my eye and heart away from my hearth after all these precious but fleeting years,' Pat says almost bleary-eyed.

'I can see that, Pat. I can indeed,' I respond in kind.

When I wake from my sad reverie, random thoughts begin to coalesce into a plan in my mind. Should I let Isabel know I've found Francesco's letter, or shall I bide my time and see if she falls for his bait? After a moment's reflection, I slide the envelope back under Isabel's pillow.

Let's just wait and see. I'll give them enough rope to hang themselves with. How could she do this to me? She's made a cuckold of me! Damn them! Damn them both! They'll pay for this, I promise. But first let me hang those *Mau Mau* terrorists tomorrow.

Chapter Twenty-Seven
Atonement Edward Nyeri Court House, 7 June 1953

I stand in my robing room and begin to contemplate which one of my garments I'm going to wear for today's final sentencing in this treason and murder trial, which is drawing to a close. I'm looking for something grand and intimidating to wear, not my usual summary court attire. Today, I'm going to pronounce the death sentence on the Robertsons' murderers and these *Mau Mau* terrorists.

Finally, I select my ceremonial high court robe to wear. It's black serge, lined with black velvet on the collar, sleeves and hem. I remove the robe from the cupboard and begin to don it carefully in front of the full-length mirror. I notice its heaviness, and soon beads of sweat began to form on my brow in this late morning tropical heat.

There's something deeply satisfying for me as I assume the persona of "Judge Stephens" in this choreographed masquerade of the law. I've always found this side of the law deeply appealing, as I can put aside my feelings and concentrate on matters of forensic evidence and law. As I think about "evidence", I pick up one of Francesco's intercepted letters from the mantelpiece and stuff into my right robe pocket.

As I place the judge's wig on my head, I feel more confident and able to do a thorough and impartial job. 'And now the *piece de resistance,*' I say to myself, as I reach into my left pocket for the black velvet head piece, which I will wear before I pronounce the death sentence. It's there. I place the square of black velvet over my wig. The image I want to create is now complete.

Standing there, looking at myself dressed for this onerous role, I remember my father telling me how it felt to preside at a court martial in the Great War; daunting but unfaltering. But I also feel a surge of vindictiveness, as I recall Isabel's last words to me: *Be careful, Ted. There'll be others in their place.* I smile at myself in the mirror at the irony of that statement, as those "others" would surely include the adulterer, Francesco. I would take great pleasure in hanging him slowly just now.

Today, however, I will focus on the law, that ineluctable force that cannot be flouted under any circumstances. The Robertsons' murderers and these *Mau Mau* terrorists will pay the final price, I think to myself. That's perfect justice. I remove the black velvet head-piece and fold it into my left pocket.

Satisfied with my attire, I approach the door of the judge's entrance and listen. I can hear the murmur and talk of nervous anticipation, and I remember that the court is unusually crowded today because of the presence of a huge contingent of Kikuyu squatters and *Mau Mau* sympathisers.

Opening the door slowly and quietly, I observe a motley collection of mostly black faces and I withdraw from the door. I walk back to the mirror, straighten my posture and observe the image of "The Honourable Judge Stephens" before me with pride.

Breathing deeply, I stride into the courtroom.

As I approach the judge's dais, the murmuring voices become subdued. The voice of the tall Sikh court usher rings out loudly, 'All rise.'

A din of feet and scraping chairs follows like a wooden chorus, as all but a handful of people rise. I make a mental note of the location of the ones in the gallery who remain seated as I step into the judge's dais.

While the courtroom audience are resettling themselves in their seats, I recall a galling phrase in Francesco's letter: *I'm so looking forward to the time when I can hold you in my arms again, and shower passionate kisses on you, my darling Isabel.*

But my vengeful thoughts are interrupted by the sound of chanting in the viewing gallery.

Some of the relatives of the arraigned prisoners start to chant the Kikuyu anthem of the *Mau Mau* freedom fighters.

The court usher thunders, 'Silence. Silence in the court,' and a few *askari* policemen begin to manhandle the protesters out of the courtroom.

'Calm yourself. Calm yourself,' I find myself muttering under my breath.

The heavy, black serge robe and wig are beginning to feel like Turkish bath towels wrapped around me in this sweltering mid-day tropical heat. I begin to mop my brow feverishly and signal to the *punkah wallah* to approach me more closely.

Once order is restored again, the usher bellows, 'The court is now in session.' As if those present were in any doubt.

The eyes of all those in the gallery and jury box turn to face me. I briefly scan the ten black men with wooden numbers around their necks in the lower dock. Sentencing these miscreants has almost become routine by now.

'Today, members of the jury, is when I shall pass judgement on the convicted felons arraigned before me. Before I do so, may I ask if there are any pleas in mitigation?'

What ensues is a shameful denial of responsibility by prisoner Mkesi who asserts, falsely of course, that he was physically coerced into signing a confession of guilt, and he even has the audacity to question my decision should I have been in his position. But I soon put an end to his specious and contemptuous questions. A Kikuyu voice breaks through clearly.

'Our comrades are innocent victims of British colonialism. We demand justice. The so-called "confessions" were obtained by torture. *Ithaka na Wiyathi!*'

The Kikuyu squatters begin to sing their anthem again, and the *askaris* sweep into the courtroom wielding batons and force the protesters outside raining blows on them as they do so.

When order is finally re-established, one and then another of Francesco's phrases blazes across my mind: *Admit it, you and he are not compatible. I've rarely met such a proud and arrogant man. I assume not all the Anglo-Irish behaves like that?*

Reaching into my left pocket, I grasp the black velvet death piece and place it carefully on my head. Turning to face the jury, I pronounce sentence.

'Gentlemen of the jury, it is the sentence of this court that the convicted felons be taken to a certain place, and then be hanged by the neck until dead.'

I turn to face the felons in the dock, and say, 'May God have mercy upon your souls.'

Cries of "Shame", "Hypocrite" and "Murderer" ring out in quick succession.

This time, the court usher and the *askaris* rush towards the protesters together and drive them out of the courtroom with flailing batons. As they are being driven out, they begin chanting the Gikuyu anthem and shouting "*Uhuru,* freedom", and "*Ithaka na Wiyathi,* Land and Freedom!"

The perspiration is streaming down my face and neck and I start to wipe them repeatedly. Despite the prevailing disarray in the courtroom, the usher shouts, 'The court is now adjourned!'

My court usher has by now partially regained his composure after losing his turban in the preceding mêlée, and bellows, 'All rise for the Honourable Judge Stephens!'

I climb out of the judge's dais and descend the stairs still wearing my "death piece". As I close the courtroom door behind me, I breathe a heavy sigh of relief and mop my forehead. After carefully folding and placing the "death piece" in my left pocket, I remove my sweat-soaked wig from my head and then reach into my right pocket to check that Francesco's letter is still there. Finally, I remove my ceremonial high court attire and hang it in my wardrobe and begin to reflect on the day's proceedings.

At last, the Robertsons' murderers and this terrorist scum have met their nemesis, and I hope it sends a clear signal to the cursed *Mau Mau* and their sympathisers: we are still in charge here.

Chapter Twenty-Eight
Wazungu Injustice Munthu and Bado

After my "confession", I am briefly allowed to meet with my kinsmen, and I discover that my treatment by the *wazungu* guards and *askaris* has been very similar to theirs. Countless people have suffered terrible tortures and starvation. Bado was one of them. One morning, they come for me in my cell, and then march me outside into the barbed wire enclosure. I can hardly stand and my eyes burn from the brightness of the sun.

'Bado, *rafikiangu,* is that you?'

He rushes up to me and we embrace. There are tears in his eyes and mine, too.

'I thought I would never see you again, Bado.'

'Don't worry*, rafikiangu*, no one can part us. You have a beard, Munthu!'

'And you also, *rafikiangu.'*

'*Una fanya nini,* what's been happening to you?' Bado asks.

'They beat me till I confessed to being responsible for the Robertson family murder,' I reply.

'*Pole,* Munthu,' Bado intones soothingly.

'*Nimeshapoa, na wewe,* and you?' I ask.

'They beat me, too, and I told them about our *Gethathi,* oath-taking ceremony. *Kabisa,* that's it,' he replies.

'*Wanna fanya nini sassa,* and now?' I ask.

'Our comrades say there will be another trial and more hangings. Many of our comrades have died this way already,' he replies.

'I see. I fear I may not see Wambui, Liza and Sam again,' I say dejectedly, and add, 'so, Bado, *rafikiangu,* can you give my beloved Wambui this *Gethiito,* lucky charm, I'm wearing as a token of my lasting love for her and our children?'

'*Ndio kabisa, rafikiangu,* I will, have no doubt,' Bado answers and adds, 'Have courage, Munthu, we will defeat these evil forces with the help of *Ngai na mababu,* God and our ancestors.'

'But will it be in time, Bado?'

'I don't know, *rafikiangu.* God willing, our fate is written.'

'*Ndio kabisa,* yes, absolutely,' I respond. There is a heavy silence between us.

After our exercise period is over, Bado and I are separated and my final memory of him is a fleeting image of his figure on the corner of the prison yard holding his right arm up with his fist clenched in the salute of our *Mau Mau* comrades shouting, '*Ithaka na Wiyathi!*'

I turn and face him and raise my right arm, shouting, '*Ithaka na Wiyathi!*'

An hour later, when the sun has captured the sky and the heat of the day in Hola Camp is like a furnace, I am summoned from my solitary cell by the *mzungu* interrogating officer and two *askaris.* The *mzungu* pushes me out of my cell and says mockingly, 'It's time to face British Justice, *Mau Mau* scum.'

After being marched across the camp, I eventually arrive in a corrugated iron shed with my tribal clan chained together. As I am pushed inside, an *askari* places a large wooden number plate around my head and neck. From now on, I lose my identity and become merely "prisoner 57". My spirits are very low, and I pray silently to *Ngai* for a swift end to this mockery of justice. What I face now, *wazungu* injustice can only have a bad outcome.

The day grows hotter and we aren't offered water to drink, so my throat feels like a desert, and our endless waiting is only relieved when groups of ten comrades are led off to the courthouse, a short walk from our metal prison. As each group of ten departs, we all sing the Gikuyu song of *Uhuru,* freedom, and are beaten for our pains by the *askaris.*

Finally, it's my turn, and I am relieved to be moving again as my legs and back feel on fire from the pain of standing in the heat and flies. I want to relieve myself but the cursed *wazungu* guards give us no privacy to do so. It's yet another painful indignity we have to endure. The ten of us with our numbers around our necks are marched along to the courthouse where we are herded into a long, narrow wooden box on the left-hand side.

As I go inside, I notice *askaris* with sticks and guns all around the walls, and sitting in the lines of chairs in front of the tallest wooden box are lines of *wazungu* who look like office workers and police. Right at the back of the court, in a separate area, are a small group of our Gikuyu women and *wazee*. They wave at us with smiling faces of encouragement, but the *askaris* nearest them begin to threaten them with their sticks.

I notice by the tallest wooden box there is a Sikh man in his turban. It reminds me of a brief visit I made to Nairobi vegetable market with my father as a boy. I wished now that I could be with my father, and with Wambui, Eliza and Sam. But it is not to be. I am suddenly jolted out of my nice memories when the Sikh shouts, 'All rise for the Honourable Judge Stephens.'

I think to myself, who is this *mzungu* who looks like a white-headed eagle in his black robe? After a while, I realise that I know this man's name. I heard from Bado that he had been Eliud's *Bwana* at Kingston Farm and I am touched by the memories and kindness of *Memsab* Stephens who listened to Bado's story about the *Mau Mau's* murder of his family, and fleeing from his village to Kingston Farm where she got him a job as house boy with the Robertson family.

If I had the choice, I would not have acted as a look-out for the *Mau Mau*. It was me or my wife and children. I feel sure that this *Bwana* Judge Stephens will not see my point of view, but I must make my case for the sake of truth and justice.

During the trial, I look at the faces of my comrades, and they betray no fear, only defiance and courage. This is what we expect of initiated men, which is what we are.

And then I hear *Bwana* judge's voice for the first time. It reminds me a little of the interrogating officer, but more superior.

'Prisoner "57", Mkesi, I have before me your signed confession informing me that you admit to murder and being a member of the *Mau Mau*, which is a proscribed organisation, and also a capital offence. Do you have anything to say in your defence?'

'*Bwana* Judge, they forced me to sign this paper!' I reply.

'What you say may or may not be true, Mkesi. However, the point is, you were acting on behalf of the *Mau Mau*, were you not?'

'I had no choice, *Bwana* Judge. They forced me to become an oath-taker, or they would kill my wife and children if I refused,' I replied.

'That is undoubtedly a lie, Mkesi. However, you have confessed to murder and joining the *Mau Mau*, which are capital offences. Do you have anything to say before I pronounce sentence?'

'*Bwana* Judge, if someone threatened to kill your wife and children, what would you do?'

'What you say, Mkesi, is contempt of this court. So now it is time to face your sentence like a man.'

'*Bwana* Judge, you *wazungu* cannot take our land. This is your crime!'

'Prisoner Mkesi, don't have the impertinence to lecture your masters!'

'But that's the truth, *Bwana* Judge.'

'The only truth I have before me is your signed confession, Mkesi.'

'But they beat me, *Bwana*! Look at me!'

Then I hear *Bwana* judge's fateful words.

'Gentlemen of the jury, it is the sentence of this court that the convicted felons be taken to a certain place, and then be hanged by the neck until dead. May God have mercy on your souls.'

"Shame…Hypocrite…Murderer", my Gikuyu countrymen and women in the court shout out.

My head is spinning and I feel sick in my stomach but try to be brave. My comrades on either side of me are shaking, waving, shouting and our chains rattle, and the last thing I remember are my tribe singing our Gikuyu *Uhuru* song, *Ithaka na Wiyathi*, as they are being attacked and driven from the courthouse. I pray to *Ngai na mababu,* God and my ancestors, to give me courage and strength to endure the ordeal that faces me now.

Chapter Twenty-Nine
Edward and Isabel 31 August 1953

I'm standing with my back to a warm wood fire in the grate while opening a telegram from Chief Justice MacDonald. The sun is setting over the purple-blues of the Mount Kenya Forest, and I feel a slight frisson of anxiety as I open this missive from my superior.

30 August 1953

Chief Justices' Office
The Supreme Court
Victoria Square
Nairobi
Kenya Colony

Dear Judge Stephens,

I am writing to inform you that in the light of resistance being offered by the indigenous tribes to Her Majesty's edict concerning the land rights of the Kikuyu and their continued breaches of Her Majesty's Peace, the government has seen fit to introduce "internment without trial".

In effect, those Kikuyu who are suspected of membership of the "Mau Mau" terrorist organisation are to be interned on suspicion of treason and will be detained pending trial and judgement. I expect you to begin the process of apprehending and detaining all those Kikuyu in your jurisdiction whom you have reasonable grounds to believe is a risk to security and Her Majesty's writ.

If you should you need additional resources to carry out this policy, please contact my assistant chief justice or chief superintendent at the above address as soon as possible.

Yours sincerely,

Sir James MacDonald
Chief Justice of the Supreme Court

I pick up the letter again and scrutinise it. My God. How on earth can MacDonald understand what it feels like to be sitting on the edge of the Mau Escarpment surrounded by rampaging and murdering *Mau Mau* burning farms and mission stations all around us? What kind of resources will it take to quell a full-scale uprising by the Kikuyu? We don't need resources, for heaven's sake, we need a battalion of British troops. Now!

Isabel walks into the living room and sees me looking upset. She comes up behind me at my desk and puts her hands on my shoulders and massages them gently.

'What's up, darling? You look anxious and upset. What's going on?' She asks me. My shoulders loosen perceptibly at Isabel's gentle, listening, touch.

'Look. I've had this ridiculous letter from Sir James, saying that we have to impose "internment without trial". It won't work and it'll antagonise the mounting fury of the Kikuyu tribes, which will then be turned against us. We're sitting ducks here, Izzy.'

'You mean Sir James wants to impose "British Justice" on the blacks, like they did on the Irish during the 1916 uprising?'

'That's about it, Izzy, but with the added risk that our whole family and household will become the target for the *Mau Mau* and every warring Kikuyu tribesman around.'

'So what'll you do, darling?'

'I'll write and ask him to reconsider the policy for the Nyeri District, or I'll threaten to resign.'

'That's a courageous decision, Ted.'

'Thanks, Izzy…Anyway, I'll give the matter some more thought before I put pen to paper.'

Looking at the picture of my father, Colonel Stephens, in the full military regalia of the Connaught Rangers on the mantelpiece, I begin to ponder before penning my letter to Sir James MacDonald.

Resigning my post is easier said than done, and I'm still in two minds about what I should do. On the one hand, I do believe that the policy is both risky and a travesty of British Justice, and on the other, I can't contemplate jeopardising my family's welfare and throwing away my promising judicial career on the grounds of principle alone. We can't just up sticks and go, can we? I need to be a little circumspect, even if Izzy doesn't fully understand.

Still, I think it's worth making the point. Here goes. I pick up my favoured fountain pen and write.

1 September 1953

District Court Offices
Delamere Street
Nyeri
Rift Valley Province

Dear Sir James,

Thank you for your letter of 30 August, which I received yesterday.

I appreciate from the content of your letter the urgency of the situation and the need to contain the growing incidence of civil unrest and acts of terrorism instigated by the "Mau Mau" terrorist organisation. In order to deal with the worsening security situation in Nyeri District, Rift Valley Province, Chief Inspector Mike Anderson and I have authorised the deployment of armed police outside all public buildings that could be at risk of attack.

However, in my opinion, the proposed policy of "internment without trial" of suspected "Mau Mau" activists and sympathises in Nyeri District will serve only to exacerbate the backlash of the terrorists and their Kikuyu supporters, which would be a grave setback to the Queen's Peace, as well as the preservation of the lives and livelihoods of vulnerable settlers and farmers living in this area.

Should you not accept my view of the situation in Nyeri District, Rift Valley Province, I regret that I may have to consider my position.

Yours sincerely,
Judge Edward Stephens

I sign the letter, fold it into an envelope and seal it with warmed wax and my signet ring. As I walk downstairs to give the letter to Juma to post, I muse, well, that's it. The die is cast, and if Sir James doesn't see matters from my point of view, I shall face a very difficult dilemma within the next day or two.

The following day, the phone rings and Juma answers it in the hallway.

'*Bwana,* telephone for you, Sir,' he says.

I'm about to leave by the front door. I stop, turn around and take the receiver from Juma's hand.

'Hello, can I help you?' I say.

'It's Sir James, Edward. I've just received your letter. Listen, Edward, you're making a grave mistake,' he says.

'I feel that I've no alternative in the circumstances, Sir James. We're sitting ducks here, and I also believe that I'm betraying the principles of British Justice if I implement "internment without trial" in these circumstances. We'll just make martyrs of them and the policy will backfire on us,' I say.

'Don't be a fool, Edward. A large contingent of British troops is on its way to you from Nairobi as we speak. And if you don't implement the policy, someone else will. Think of your wife and family. Can you afford to go home dishonoured and without a posting?' Sir James asks pointedly. There's a poignant silence.

My God, he's right, what the hell can we do without another posting and our livelihood? I can't just abandon my family and career. I must have been mad to even consider this course of action.

'I'll think about what you've said, Sir James,' I reply.

'You do that, Edward. Ring me at six o'clock this evening,' Sir James concludes.

'I shall. Thank you for ringing, Sir James,' I reply, replacing the receiver.

There's still time to consider my position, thank God. But what'll I tell Izzy?

No doubt, she'll say I'm a coward and a pawn of the colonial British government and its corrupt legal system. But have I any real choice? Doesn't she see the enormity of the situation I'm in, and its serious consequences for us all? Someone has to behave responsibly.

Juma has been listening to this conversation from the servant's entrance. He quietly opens the kitchen door and slips within. I take a deep breath, walk back to the front door and leave Kingston Farm for the district court in Nyeri.

When I come home from the court later that evening, Isabel meets me on the veranda. Pouring me a glass of whisky, she asks, 'So, my darling, what have you decided to do about Sir James?'

'I've been thinking about what he said, and he's right. How can we afford to return to England without the prospect of another posting?'

'So you've backed down, have you?'

'Not really. I've decided to put our family and our livelihood first.'

'Have you no courage and integrity, Ted?'

'How dare you talk to me about integrity? It's you that's been having an affair with Senor Francesco do Nascimento behind my back and lying to me all the while.'

'What…what are you talking about, Ted?' Isabel asks anxiously, backing away from me.

'Don't lie to me anymore, Izzy. I found one of Francesco's letters under your pillow weeks ago. And I've other proofs of your betrayal.'

'What do you mean? What betrayal and what…proofs are you talking about, Ted?'

'I'm not prepared to say right now,' I reply coldly.

'And yet you're prepared to betray your precious principles of "British Justice" to save your skin.'

'That's a mean lie. I'm saving all our skins by not resigning. Can't you bloody well see that?'

'That's a cop out, Ted.'

'Damn you to Hell!' I say finally.

I storm out of the living room, slamming the door behind me.

Isabel

Cleo and Rex stir anxiously in front of the fire, and Isabel bursts into floods of choking tears. They go over to her and begin to nuzzling her legs. When her tears eventually subside, Isabel begins to reflect on her situation.

My God. What am I going to do now? He's read that letter and knows Francesco and I had an affair. What else does he know, for Christ's sake? I pray he that doesn't also know the truth about Robert. I retreat to the marital bedroom, lie down on the bed and cry. Exhausted, I fall into a deep slumber, and begin dreaming of what I've been doing to conceal Robert's true heritage since his birth.

I'm in our bathroom at Kingston Farm, and Robert is sitting up in his white enamel bath playing with the bubbles and his carved balsa wood lifeboat that bobs up and down in the miniature wave-tossed sea. He's gurgling away happily and I'm singing Oh for the Days of the Kerry Dancing, *one of his favourite tunes.*

On the floor by the bath is a small bottle of Hydrogen Peroxide, a bowl and a sponge. While Robert's distracted playing with his boat and my singing, I soak the sponge in the chemical and begin dabbing it on to his wet hair which is beginning to show the tell-tale signs of black hair coming through his beautifully soft scalp, which I know to be Francesco's legacy and our undoing.

'Oh Christ, may Ted never discover the truth of dear Robert's parentage or we're done for,' I say to myself in between the refrain of Kerry Dancing. *If only I hadn't been so foolhardy when I was with Francesco in London in the spring of 1951.*

Edward

When I return home that evening, there is a palpable coldness and distance between Isabel and I. And later that night, as I wrestle with my insomnia, I begin to dream.

I'm floating out of control and being buffeted by hurricane winds. There are glaciers and mountains towering above and all around me. I scream in fear of my life as I drift helplessly underneath the lowering and maddening sky. There are irresistible currents pulling me towards the rocky crags and trees. I skim the grey and green perils as they sweep beneath my feet.

I'm falling...losing control. And suddenly, I'm in flames like a butterfly aflame in a forest fire. I reach my arm over to find Izzy. But she's gone!

Chapter Thirty
Isabel Kingston Farm, 3 September 1953

I'm standing in front of the wardrobe in our dressing room and I'm trying to decide what to wear for my journey to Nairobi. I couldn't sleep very well after our row, and then I woke dreaming of Elena going around the farm holding a lighted candle.

All around her were threatening shadows armed with machetes. There was an uncontrollable fire and everyone was burned to death.

I'm shaking with cold in the chill morning air of the White Highlands. In front of me is a range of tropical suits that Ted bought at "Lilywhites" in the Haymarket before we travelled out to Kenya at the start of our first posting to Nyeri, when my mind and heart were filled with the joy of travel, adventure and infinite possibilities.

Now, it's different. The array of Ted's judicial garments resembles a priest's vestibule, in a curious way. There's something of atonement in it all. I can see him standing there in front of the full-length mirror wearing all his court finery and rehearsing his opening remarks like the fine orator and judge he is. I never imagined that one day, he would be sitting in judgement of me. My da was right:

'If you marry a judge, my darling, you marry the system,' he said.

'Here it is,' I say to myself as I remove my tropical khaki suit from its hanger and hold it against myself in front of the mirror.

This is how I was dressed as we set off from the British high commissioner's office in Nairobi that beginning of June eighteen months ago full of anticipation and hope of our new posting. And now look at us. God! What's that noise? It must be the hyenas ravaging the buffalo that was killed by a lion yesterday.

It reminds me of that Masai warrior we stopped for on our first journey to Nyeri who had been attacked by a lion. So much has happened since then. I can still remember parts of our conversation that day.

'Stop!' I shouted. 'Someone's hurt.'

Ted slowed the car and pulled in to the side of the road. He hadn't noticed him at all. Standing there was tall, young, lean, red and black Masai warrior dressed in a long, brown blood-spattered sarong, and holding a wood and iron spear in his left, uninjured, hand. His right arm hung limply by his side and his upper body was covered in caked and congealed blood, with folds of exposed flesh attracting a swarm of flies.

'Wenda wapi?' Ted asked the young warrior.

Where are we going? All our hopes are dashed now, and we have no future here in Kenya. Our time is up. I reach up into the wardrobe again and take hold of my Stetson, and as I do so, my arm brushes against Ted's black, velvet-edged robe. Out of morbid curiosity, I put that cumbrous garment on laboriously and look at myself in the mirror. As I stare unblinkingly at my image, I feel a rising sense of shame and bewilderment.

Here I am, an IRA man's daughter, wearing a British judge's robes. I must be out of my mind. I've finally lost it. How have I created this madness? Da was right, after all.

I put my hand into the right hand pocket of the black velvet robe, and find a letter. I unfold it and read it in the dawn light. It's one of Francesco's letters. I can't quite believe this nightmare is happening to me. And just to be sure, I reach into the left-hand pocket and find Ted's "death piece". I am condemned.

I sink to my knees and bury my face in my hands and sob uncontrollably. Finally, I get up slowly and it dawns on me that I have to put as much distance between Ted and myself as I can. But I'm taking Robert with me, whatever happens.

The Nyeri-Nairobi Road

The dawn air is licked gently with the sweet dampness of Highland mist and dew, and on either side of the red laterite road, there are zebras grazing and gazelle mingling innocently among them. The scorching African sun is already burning off the mist, revealing *Kere Nyaga,* with its peaks enshrouded in clouds on the horizon.

I'm in a Peugeot Taxi heading back to Nairobi from Nyeri. I left with Robert and a suitcase before the sun rose at six o'clock. Elena gave me a warm farewell embrace, and wished me *safari njema.* She said that she would come and visit me in Nairobi when she can. I shall miss her support, and so will Robert.

I'm left with plaintive echoes of Cleo and Rex barking as the taxi bounces erratically down the pot-holed Nairobi road, and I feel an unfamiliar lightness and freedom while Robert's head lies on my breast. He's asleep at last, thank God.

Chapter Thirty-One
Edward Kingston Farm, 3 September 1953

I wake to find Izzy gone and feel sick to my stomach. I'm like that helpless butterfly blown into the inferno that I dreamed of last night. A part of me wants to curl up and die, and the other part wants to punish Izzy severely for betraying and leaving me. I look around the bedroom and dressing room, and scattered all over the place are piles of clothes discarded in Izzy's desperate rush to escape.

It resembles the scene of a crime. What am I going to do now? I'm painfully reminded about the day my mother sent me away to boarding school when I was six, and once again, I realise that women are not to be trusted.

I can hear my governesses' voice: *'It's about school.'*

'What about school?'

'You're getting to the age when you really should be thinking about going, you know.'

'But I thought you were my teacher, Katie, and I'm studying hard, aren't I?'

'Of course you are, Eddy. But that's not the point.'

'What is the point, Katie.'

'The point is that your mother and father have suggested it's time you went to boarding school.'

I couldn't quite believe what I was hearing and had to really focus my mind.

'What's the point of boarding school, Katie? I'm learning all I need to here with you, aren't I?'

'The thing is, Eddy, your mum and Dad want you to mix with other children, so you can make friends and gain confidence.'

'I'm quite happy here, Katie, and I have all the friends I need here!'

'Who do you mean?'

'Well, "Mischief" for a start. And what will happen to him if I go to boarding school. Who will look after him?'

'I'm sure "Mischief" will be properly cared for. But aren't you lonely for other boys' company sometimes?'

'No, not at all. I'm quite happy with the way things are, thank you.'

'Well, Eddy, this isn't the way your parents see things at present, I'm afraid.'

'Will you not make my case for me, Katie? After all, I'm a good student, aren't I? And you'll miss me, won't you?'

'You are a good student, Eddy, and of course I shall miss you when you go to boarding school. We all will.'

With those words I felt that Katie had capitulated to my parents.

I was standing in front of my mother and father who were sitting in their favourite settee in the living room with the late afternoon sun streaming in bearing the reflected images of the thorny roses lining the windows and yellowing autumn leaves.

'So Edward, I believe Katie has spoken to you of the plans for you to attend the Oratory School in London, has she not,' my father said.

'Well, yes, father, but I'm happy learning my lessons here with Katie.'

'Listen, Eddy. Can't you see how important it is for you to be with your peers, learning and playing alongside them?' My mother interjected.

'How can you acquire the self-confidence you will need in life if you spend all your time with the animals in the fields?' Father said.

For a moment I was tongue-tied, and felt the heat rising from under my shirt collar, reddening my face.

'But who will look after Mischief and the dogs, Father?'

'We will, of course, Eddy. Have no fear of that,' he replied.

With those words, I knew that my fate had been sealed.

I shout, 'Elena. *Kuja hapa. Haraka*, come here. Hurry!'

There's a troubling silence. I call out again, and finally Juma appears.

'*Wapi*, where's Elena?'

'Elena *a nyumbani*, Bwana. Her mother is ill.'

'Is that so?'

'*Kweli*, really, Bwana.'

I don't believe a word of it.

I throw my clothes on and go downstairs to the front porch of Kingston Farm. As I stand there in the crisp and rapidly brightening African dawn, I observe a group of vultures circling overhead. I reckon that our ungraceful visitors were waiting till the hyenas had done their work on the remains of the buffalo that had been killed by lions last night.

I dearly wish it had been fragments of Francesco's corpse that the vultures were waiting for. I take a deep breath of the dew-filled African air, and call Cleo and Rex to my side. They both rush at me from the front lawn, beating my thighs with their tails and burying their noses in my crotch in a re-assuring and friendly way.

'Where's Izzy, then? *Wenda wapi Memsab?* Tell me, where did she go?'

'I'm sure you weren't part of her conspiracy, were you?' That's for sure.

'Let's bring her back, shall we? Let's bring her back home to Kingston Farm. What do you think?'

Cleo and Rex bark in seeming agreement, and rush away over the front lawn in search of their mistress. After packing a small overnight holdall, I lock the front door to Kingston Farm and clamber into my station wagon. Before I drive away, I instruct Juma to look after Cleo and Rex, and the farm, and put extra armed guards on the entrance.

'*Safari njema*, safe journey, *Bwana*,' Juma says. 'I hope you find your wife and son, *Bwana.*'

'*Asante sana na kwaheri*, thank you and goodbye, Juma,' I reply.

'*Kwaheri, Bwana.* Goodbye and may *Ngai* go with you.'

Cleo and Rex bark and chase the station wagon all the way to the end of the drive to Kingston Farm. As the red dust thrown up by the retreating station wagon begins to settle, I look in the rear view mirror and see Juma waiting patiently for Cleo and Rex to return. As I'm travelling on the erratically pot-holed Nyeri-Nairobi road in pursuit of Izzy, I begin rehearsing the various consequences of her foolhardy flight to Nairobi and the arguments I will use to bring her back home.

What am I going to say to her when I eventually find her? I mustn't let my anger get the better of me, whatever happens. Yet I'm furious with her. Not only has she cuckolded me in the eyes of the world, but she has also left me with doubts about the legitimacy of Robert. A passage of Francesco's letter comes to me with this thought. *Admit it, you and Edward are not compatible, whereas you and I are on the same wavelength. We're ordinary mortals with artists' souls and a passion for life.*

A passion for adultery, you mean. My stomach turns when I remember the image of her "best man", Francesco de Nascimento, arm in arm with her at our wedding. I had been entirely hoodwinked by them both. Finally, I recall the *coup de grace* in Francesco's letter:

Your life would have been very different here with me in London if you hadn't got engaged and married to Edward and gone to live in your little town in Africa.

I find it hard to focus on the road to Nairobi, which is being washed away in the sudden tropical downpour enveloping my station wagon. Red mud, churned up from the shifting laterite road, spatters the windscreen making visibility nigh impossible.

Through the brief intermittent swipes of the blades, I notice the loping giraffes and attendant zebras grazing on the savannah receding into the sheet-grey monsoon rains sweeping across the gently rolling White Highlands. In the hazy distance, I can see clumps of thatched huts near the edge of the road and can smell cooking smoke emerging from their ridges. There's certainly a strange beauty here.

Chapter Thirty-Two
Izzy Royal Victoria Hotel, Muthaiga, Nairobi, 20 October 1953

I'm lying in a hot bath singing one of my favourite operatic arias from "La Traviata", "Libiamo", "the Drinking Song". And I have a vivid memory when I first saw this opera with Francesco. I'm outside the opera house waiting for Francesco and admiring all these fine ladies and gentlemen. What seems to be a very popular outfit among the ladies is knee-length purple or black silk dresses graced with a range of attractive feather boas.

And they all have high-heeled Italian shoes and splendidly exotic handbags to match. I can't quite see dear Ted forking out for such an outfit for me in Dublin, alas.

Now I hear his voice.

'Ah, Isabella, so here you are!' He greets me with open arms and a gentle kiss on both cheeks.

'Hello, Francesco! I've been looking out for you,' I reply.

'Me too!' He says.

I notice Francesco studying my outfit in an unobtrusive way, which pleases me. I'm wearing my red high-heeled Italian shoes, a lilac and purple evening gown and silk scarf, and my prettiest blue velvet overcoat.

'You do look most delightful tonight, Isabella, I must say.'

'Thank you, Francesco,' I say with a beaming smile, acknowledging that not only is Francesco a cultured man, but also very attuned to feminine ways.

'Come, I have our tickets, Isabella. Let's go and find our box,' he says, as he takes me gently by my arm and steers me past the dense crowd of opera-lovers around us.

I had heard so much about the Royal Opera House from Ted, who told me he used to come here with his parents when they visited London in the late 30s.

A love of opera is something both Ted and Francesco share, except Dublin can't compete with London's Royal Opera House, which is a shame. Francesco shows me into our seats, which are to the upper left wing of the stage. Perfect for sight and sound, I imagine.

As I'm surveying the opulent crowd, Francesco asks me, 'Isabella, do you know the libretto *of "La Traviata"?' From what Ted told me, I think he means the story.*

'I'm afraid I don't, but perhaps you can enlighten me?'

'Indeed, I will.'

As we are sitting in our balcony seats, I can see that our view of the stage is perfect, and all around us we can see the social elite of London in all their show and opulence. Ted would have approved of this audience greatly, I'm sure.

'Well, let me summarise the plot of "La Traviata" for you, Isabella, in one paragraph,' Francesco says leaning towards me, and I can smell his exotic musk after shave.

'Please do.'

'Well, Violetta, the main protagonist, falls in love with a wealthy young man, Alfredo, and he wishes to marry her, but she is an unsuitable match for him. His father, Geraldo, persuades her to relinquish her affections, which leaves them both broken-hearted.'

'How very sad.'

'But isn't all opera, my dear?'

'I suppose you're right, Francesco. Opera always seems to end in blood and tears.'

'Indeed, it does, Isabella.'

In my musings, I sometimes think that opera does in fact mirror life when it comes to the sphere of human emotions, and that's why we're so often drawn to its powerful mirroring in our own lives The orchestra are still fine tuning themselves, and I do love the sounds of violins and flutes, with their gentle harmonic interplay.

As the lights go down, the orchestra begins to play a lively waltzing tune, and when the curtain lifts, we are presented with a magnificent sight of a court ball, with finely dressed ladies and gentlemen dancing together in lines. I'm in suspended animation with all this heavenly music around me, and yet a fleeting pang of guilt floats across my heart as I think of Ted, and our first romantic

107

musical evening together in Dublin. I turn to look at Francesco's profile, and as I do so, he catches my eye and smiles warmly. I return his smile.

'Isn't "Libiamo", the "Drinking Song" so delightful?' He says.

'Tis, and I love the way that Violetta and Alfredo sing it with such passion,' I reply.

The first act of "La Traviata" unfolds with constant protestations of everlasting love, and I now regret that I can almost foresee the inevitable frustration of Violetta and Alfredo's situations. As the second act of the opera proceeds, I have a strong sense of their doomed relationship, and I recall a conversation between my da and Ma, when I was still living at home in Dublin. It was the first time I admitted my love for Ted to my da, after we had finished dinner, and Ma was in the kitchen and it was just Da and me.

'Da, I'm in love with Ted.'

'So why choose Ted when you could find one of your own?'

'Love chooses us, Da. You know that.'

Well, perhaps you're right there, Izzy.'

'Will you give us your blessing, Da?'

'On two conditions, Izzy.'

'What are they?'

'You'll let me tell your mother, as you know how sensitive she is about these matters, and secondly, you agree to bring up any children you have in the Catholic faith.'

'Of course, Da, I'm happy to agree to both conditions.'

'So be it, then, my darling Izzy. I give you both my blessing.'

After the final act of "La Traviata" came to its tearful and tragic end, I couldn't help but shed a few tears for all that unrequited love, at which point Francesco put his left arm around my shoulders and held me for a while. I didn't resist his sympathetic and gentle touch.

'Come,' Francesco said, 'let me find a cab for us,' he offered.

When we arrived at his sequestered apartment in Belgravia, Francesco said, 'Isabella, you are most welcome to come in and have a little nightcap with me, if you like?'

Suddenly, I hear a knock on my bedroom door.

Knock. Knock.

'Who's that?' I shout, getting out of the bath.

'It is Elena, *Memsab*.'

'*Kuja hapa,* come in, Elena.'

'What news of *Bwana* Edward?' I ask as I admit Elena into the lounge wearing my bath robe.

'Juma told me that *Bwana* Edward is angry with you because you ran away from Kingston Farm. He said that he is going to bring you back, *Memsab.*'

'I see. So who is looking after Cleo and Rex on the farm?' I ask.

'Juma is looking after the dogs, *Memsab.*'

'That's good…Robert has missed your cuddles, Elena.'

'*Kweli*, really, *Memsab*. He is used to me,' Elena laughs.

'*Asante sana*, thank you for all your help with him, Elena.'

'*Hata kidogo*, you are welcome, *Memsab.*'

'I've left a letter on the dressing table for *Bwana* Edward. I believe he's staying at the Muthaiga Club. Please see he gets it, Elena. *Asante sana.*'

'*Ndio, Memsab,*' Elena replies. '*Kwaheri, Memsab.*'

'*Kwaheri,* Elena.'

After Elena leaves, I climb out of my bathrobe and don my dressing robe. Walking over to Robert's cot, I watch him sleeping peacefully after a long and restless night. I pick him up and hold him to my chest. As I settle down on the ottoman, the hot dry winds of the Nairobi Plateau blow-dry my hair through the mosquito screen beside me, and I begin to reflect on the turn of events since leaving Kingston Farm six weeks ago.

Ted's fury has probably abated by now, I hope. How could I have ever imagined that dyeing Robert's hair could have concealed his true origins? He's got Francesco's colouring to begin with. If Ted knows, he's left with the decision to accept or reject us both. I regret my stupidity but not the birth of this precious and lovely boy.

The alternatives are too terrible to think about. If Ted does reject us both, I'm faced with the dreadful prospect of returning to Dublin in shame and disgrace. Ma and Da would never welcome me back, I know. And I can never admit the truth to them. The thought of that is too awful to contemplate. Somehow I've got to find a way forward that will enable us all to thrive.

I recall a conversation I had with Ted a few years after the after the war when we were courting.

It was a wet autumn night and we were having our first anniversary dinner at Switzer's Restaurant in Grafton Street having just returned from seeing Sean O'Casey's wonderful play at the Abbey Theatre: "Juno and the Paycock".

'So, Ted, what did you think of Sean O'Casey's play, then?'

'Well, it certainly had spirit, humour and a bucketful of realism. What did you think, Izzy?'

'I really enjoyed it, particularly the farcical goings on between Captain Jack and Joxer.'

'Do you think it represented the real issues to do with the strike in the 1930s?'

'Yes, I thought the worker's case was well represented by O'Casey.'

'I'm not sure Juno would have agreed with that!'

'You mean as the main breadwinner?'

'Absolutely!'

At this point, the waiter comes up to Ted and Isabel's table and offers them the wine menu, standing between Ted and Isabel expectantly.

'Don't worry, you needn't wait, we'll just need a minute,' *says Ted politely.*

'What do you fancy for a drink, Izzy?'

'Shall we order a bottle of the "Chateau de Neuf Pape"?'

'I'm not so sure, Izzy. Can you see the price tag?'

A frown appears on Isabel's face, which Ted tries to ignore.

'I say, why we don't go for the French house wine. I've heard it's good here.'

'Well, if you like,' *Isabel concedes reluctantly.*

I'm thinking to myself, how is it that this handsome and talented man I love so dearly, with all his class upbringing should be so stingy when it comes to spending a little money and just enjoying a nice time occasionally. After all, it is our anniversary.

After the house wine has arrived, and Isabel and Ted are somewhat "in vino veritas", Edward says, 'I think the issue of Mary's shame is also a powerful sub-plot, don't you?'

'Yes, I can't imagine what she'll do carrying Bentham's illegitimate child like that.'

'I guess it'll spell the end of all her prospects after that,' *Ted says.*

'Without doubt,' *I agree.*

A part of me also thinks what double standards men have about the consequences of their folly. So I can't help adding, 'However, it does seem to me that Bentham, the stupid lawyer, gets away lightly.'

'But isn't that always the case, my darling?'

A part of me is shamed and angry into admitting the truth of our patriarchal, Catholic values.

'I guess so,' I say finally.

Our dinner conversation strays into less controversial subjects after this, which I'm relieved about. I should have heeded my da's good advice: "Izzy, whatever you do in polite society, never talk about sex, religion or politics".

I could return to London and seek Francesco's protection and patrimony, but I know that it would destroy any hope of reconciliation with Ted and my parents in the long run. As a last resort, I could always sit it out here in Nairobi and try to make a go of my plans for a hat and dress-making business, "*La Coquette*". But that might create a terrible scandal for Ted and me, eventually. At least I've got these skills to fall back on should everything go pear-shaped.

As I consider these dilemmas, I remember the moving scene in "*La Traviata*" in which Violetta admits her love for Alfredo to his father, Geraldo, and I hum the tune. As I do so, I know in my heart, I'm not ready to let go of Ted.

Chapter Thirty-Three
Edward Muthaiga Club, Nairobi,
23 October 1953

The stifling air of the Muthaiga Club in Nairobi has the redolence of cigars, beer and ageing spirits. After all, it was in this clubhouse, thirty years before, that the same breed of starched, misogynistic colonials toasted the famed Baroness von Blixen (Isak Dinesen), author of *Out of Africa*. Nothing has changed. The club still boasts the haughty, seven feet tall, turbaned Pathan waiters who symbolise the vanished Empire of India, and which accentuates Kenya's faltering colonial future since the *Mau Mau* uprising began.

I've just arrived hot foot from Nyeri on one of my repeated searches for Izzy. As I scan the crowd of faces looking for a confidante to talk to, I notice a tall, dark-haired, ascetic-looking man whom I know.

'Hello, Charles. How are you?' I ask.

'Ted, how are you, old chap?'

'Could be better, Charles. Life's murder at present.'

'Sorry to hear it. What's up?'

I mop my perspiring brow and neck with my handkerchief and look around self-consciously.

'Is there somewhere we can talk privately?'

'Sure. Let's go out on to the veranda.'

'OK,' I concur.

As we stand on the veranda overlooking the well-irrigated and manicured lawns of the Muthaiga Club, the rural squalor and isolation of Nyeri seems far away from my mind.

'So, tell me, what's up?' Charles asks.

'Izzy's left me and taken my son.'

'You can't be serious?'

'I am.'

'Where's she now?'

'I've finally tracked her down to the Royal Victoria…'

'And so what are you going to do?'

I avert my eyes from Charles' concerned gaze and focus on the perimeter of palm trees, through which the diffuse and setting rays of the African sun are shining.

'I'm going to confront her tomorrow and sort this.'

'What's it all about, Ted, if you don't mind me asking?'

'Well, it's a long story, Charles. Let's just say that she's behaved…scandalously.'

I hold on tightly to the balustrade to prevent my hands shaking uncontrollably.

'In what way?' Charles enquires.

'I'd rather not talk about the details, if…'

'Sure, I understand. When are you going to join us for our next game of polo, Ted? There's a match on Saturday. Are you up for it?' Charles asks.

'Thanks for the invitation. I'd love to, Charles, but I must…'

'Don't worry. I do understand,' says Charles.

I remove my white sports cap from my head and run my fingers through my sweat-soaked hair and scalp.

'Thanks for listening, Charles. I really appreciate it. I'll be in touch…'

'That's fine, Ted. Don't forget: keep your pecker up, old chap, and if you change your mind about the polo match this Saturday, you'll know where to find us,' says Charles reassuringly, as he disappears into the cigar and whisky fug of the Muthaiga Club.

Chapter Thirty-Four
Edward Royal Victoria Hotel, Muthaiga,
24 October 1953

The sprinklers on the Royal Victoria Hotel lawns are spinning crazily in the scorching heat of the mid-day sun as I mount the stairs to the terrace and reception area. Surveying the opulent splendour of my surroundings, I wonder in whose name Izzy has registered at the hotel. Will she have used her maiden name to conceal her identity, or will she have used her married name in order to bill the expenses to me?

Walking into the darkened reception area, I note the array of forlorn trophies of game hunters that adorn the striated, velvet walls of this Edwardian hotel. One of them catches my eye. It is the stuffed head of a leopard with gleaming canines and glassy eyes. Grimacing and sparkling, but lifeless.

'Good day, Sir. How can I help you?' The Indian receptionist asks.

'I've come to see Mrs Stephens,' I reply.

'I believe you are being expected, Sir. Room 224, turn right through the double door.'

'Thank you,' I reply.

As I trudge up the stairs to the second floor of the hotel, I rehearse all the arguments I will use to persuade Izzy to return to Kingston Farm, the chief of which is the avoidance of scandal for a man in my position. I knock on her door.

'Hello. Who is it?' Izzy asks.

'It's me. Ted,' I reply.

The door opens to reveal Izzy dressed in her khakis over a light blue cotton blouse unbuttoned to her collarbones, which are moist with perspiration.

'Do come in, Ted. It's good to see you,' she says.

'It's good to see you, too, Izzy,' I reply as I look into Izzy's eyes, searching for some signs of contrition or even affection for me in her gaze. There are none, only apprehension.

'So what have you to say for…'

'You know exactly why I left.'

'There was no need to disappear like a thief in the night.'

Izzy averts her gaze and steps sideways.

'Ted, I couldn't stand it anymore. Your uncontrollable rages are terrifying…'

'Well, what do you expect with your unforgivable…'

'You behave like a brute, Ted.'

'So it's my entire fault, is it? What kind of man do you think I am?'

Isabel steps backwards a pace and holds on to the bedstead for support. Taking a deep breath and gathering herself, she responds, 'You see what I mean? We can't carry on like this. I'm not prepared to live like a tortured criminal anymore, Ted. I'm your wife, and I'm sorry for what I did in a moment of foolhardy weakness…'

'Dadee, Mumee, Dadee!'

'Where's Robert?' I ask, looking past Izzy.

'He's sleeping next door. He's been very restless and disturbed since we left the farm.'

I turn away from Izzy and walk to the adjoining bedroom and open the door. As I approach Robert's cot, I gaze at the sprawled and elongated body of this sallow, black-haired boy. Picking him up gently from the cot, Robert snuggles into my shoulder and murmurs sleepily, 'Dada. Dada.'

Izzy follows me into Robert's room and stands facing us.

'So, Izzy, what are you suggesting as a way forward?'

'I think it's best that Robert and I come back to the farm, and see if we can live peacefully, like…

'Are you sure that's what you want, Izzy?'

'I'm sure. And I'm truly sorry for what happened, Ted.'

Izzy moves towards me slowly as I put my free arm around her lightly. We embrace.

'Dada, Mama, Dada,' Robert says quietly, as if to himself.

Chapter Thirty-Five
Edward A Game for Mounted Gentlemen

Across the expanse of green lawns and fenced enclosures could be heard the sounds of clattering sticks, shouts of exhortation and jubilation as white garbed men mounted on polo ponies charged hither and thither in pursuit of a small leather ball and a goal. Despite the tribulations of waning empire and domestic dilemmas, the colonial gentry always found time to indulge their passion for horses, balls and winning.

I was feeling greatly relieved that Izzy had finally agreed to come home with Robert to Kingston Farm avoiding further scandal and embarrassment, which put me in a good mood for a game.

'Hi, Ted, so glad you could make it!' Charles shouted out from the practise field where he was putting "Shannon", his cross-Arab polo pony, through her warm-up exercises.

'So am I, Charles!' I replied, waving at him as I made my way over to the stables to prepare and saddle "Mischief".

As I walked into the stable yard, I could smell the pungent aroma of horses' urine, mixed with straw and saddle soap. The Indian grooms were conscientiously sweeping and washing out the stables, as I entered Mischief's stall. He was neighing with excitement as I approached him. After all, it had been some months since I had seen or ridden him and we were mutually excited to be in each other's company again.

'Well, dear Mischief, how've you been, then, eh?'

He put his muzzle up to my nose and we exchanged breath.

'Good, eh? That's good to know.'

We continued our silent exchange with me stroking his excited neck and him nuzzling my left ear.

'Okay, let's saddle-up, shall we?'

I went into Mischief's stall, gave him a quick groom, checking his hooves as I did so.

'You're in fine fettle today, aren't you?'

He replied by pushing me away playfully.

'Yes, you are, yes you are,' I replied putting his saddle on and tightening the girth straps.

As I walk Mischief out into the yard and through the stable yard, I feel that living here near Muthaiga and Nairobi would be a safer option than being in Nyeri and the haunts of the *Mau Mau*. However, after my last issue with Chief Justice MacDonald, I think it's wiser for me to just hang on in Nyeri for the time being.

Soon, I'm mounted on Mischief's supple and muscular back and joining Charles in the practise field where we ride around hitting the chuck to each other for our warm-up.

'So who are we up against today, Charles?'

'We're playing the Kampala Officer's Club, who have quite a fierce reputation I gather,' he replies.

'Okay, let's give them a run for their money, shall we?'

With that response, we both head out into the arena and line up for the fray. The upshot of our closely fought game is that we are narrowly beaten by "the Officers" due to one of our champion players being injured in a bad fall. As I come out of the arena, I give Mischief a lot of fuss, and tell him he gave of his best, as usual, and I walk him around the stable yard to help cool himself down before I give him over to the groom.

'Thanks for reminding me about the match, Charles, and let's hope we settle scores with the "Kampala Officer's Club" next time,' I say.

'You bet, Ted, and it's good to see you and Mischief back in action again after such a long spell.'

As I drove out of Muthaiga Polo Club, I waved goodbye to Charles and our mutual friends and headed off to the Royal Victoria Hotel to collect Izzy and Robert.

'Now it's back to the front line,' I say to myself as I head back to Kingston Farm.

Chapter Thirty-Six
Mayhem Kingston Farm, 4 December 1953

It was a full moon, and the tree frogs, crickets and hyenas were in a clamorous mood. Yet gathered around the magistrate's house was a sombre collection of beings. Some were dressed in leopard skins over their heads and shoulders and carried long, razor-covered poles, while others were dressed in discarded police shirts and khakis and carried machetes and spears.

First, it was the turn of the "fish-hookers". They crept towards the house crouching like the leopards they mimicked, stalking their prey. As they reached the barred windows in the front of the house, they inserted their lethal rods and began fishing for glittering prizes from the judge's house.

While the "fish-hookers" busied themselves with their household plunder, the machete-carrying warriors began to scale the cedar tree that overhung the house. One by one, they dropped stealthily on to the first floor veranda and took up siege positions outside the bedrooms. At the sound of a prearranged whistle, they began a full-scale assault on the windows.

The sounds of splintering glass and smashed wood woke Cleo and Rex, who began barking madly and rushing upstairs. Then the screaming began, desperate and piercing.

'Mummeee...Dadeee...Mummee!' Robert's screaming could be clearly heard above the din of crazed barking, cursing and smashing glass.

All at once, Edward and Isabel shook themselves from their sleep, grabbed their revolvers from under their pillows and fled to Robert's bedroom. As soon as Edward entered the room, he started to fire his revolver randomly at the windows and curses of pain could be heard in response.

'Damn you, bloody bastards. I'll kill all of you if I have to. Die, die, die,' he shouted as he fired repeatedly.

The marauders were beaten back in a hail of bullets and they dropped and fell from the veranda, and disappeared crippled or limping into the forest's edge. Cleo and Rex went in hot pursuit of the invaders, but reluctantly gave up the chase after sustaining machete wounds to their flanks.

'It's all right, my darling, it's all right. They've gone now. They've gone. You'll be all right. It's all right now,' Isabel said as she tried to comfort Robert's frantic screaming and holding him close to her chest.

'Mumee, Mumee!' Robert continued to wail.

Edward was already downstairs in the lobby and talking to Inspector Anderson on the phone.

'I don't care how few armed police you have in reserve. Just get them here. Quickly!'

A short pause followed.

'I guess there were about twenty *Mau Mau* in all, mostly armed with spears and machetes...Sure, we'll sit tight till they get here. I'm not taking chances. Okay, see you shortly.'

Edward replaces the receiver and goes to comfort Isabel and Robert. Isabel is back in their bedroom holding Robert tightly as they both lie on the bed. Edward goes up to them and sits on the edge of the bed reaching out his right arm, making contact with Robert's shoulders which are shaking with shock.

'Don't worry, Robert, it'll be okay. The police are on their way and the terrorists are all gone now.'

'How long did Anderson say they will be?' Izzy asks anxiously.

'About half an hour,' Edward replies.

'Thank God. I really can't live here anymore, Ted. It's far too dangerous for us all.'

'I'm beginning to agree with you, Izzy. I really am.'

Chapter Thirty-Seven
Edward Nyeri Court House,
5 December 1953

It was a dry and unforgivingly hot day as Judge Edward Stephens stood in the ante-chamber of the magistrate's court in Nyeri facing Chief of Police, Mike Anderson.

'I don't give a damn,' said Edward.

'They brought it on themselves and now they deserve everything we can throw at them.'

'But there isn't enough room in the detention camps for all the suspected terrorists we've rounded up already, Ted.'

'They can go and live in the forests they originally came from for all I care.'

'As you wish,' Anderson replied, as he left Judge Stephens brooding at his desk.

We've been far too soft on them so far. That's going to change from now on. Never mind intern them. Shoot them all, is what I say. If we don't crush this rebellion outright, British rule in Kenya will be over in a matter of a few months. I'm going home now to have a serious talk with Isabel about our security situation in this terrifying escalation of Kikuyu violence and rebellion.

However, political commentators from all sides began to ponder the wisdom and legitimacy of British policies in Kenya that involved atrocities and reprisals on both sides. An up and coming journalist, James Cameron, wrote a poignant and critical eye-witness article in a national newspaper about the massacre of twenty Kikuyu civilians by B Company of the 5th Kenya African Rifles in June 1953. His conclusion was:

Britain neither knows nor cares anything for the white man's burden in Kenya (The Age, December 1953).

Upstairs in my study at Kingston Farm, I reflect that this was the second time that Kingston Farm had been attacked. The first time, the *Mau Mau* claimed the life of our gardener, Eliud, and last night, they nearly succeeded in massacring us all. That's it, I've decided I've got to protect Izzy and Robert, and it will be safer for them both in Nairobi until we quell this rebellion. I'll have a talk with her in the nursery.

I find Izzy downstairs in the drawing room bathed in the bright African sun streaming through the open windows billowing with fresh air from the beckoning slopes of Mount Kenya in the background. She is squatting on the floor opposite Robert, who is waiting for her to roll his ball.

'What is it, Ted? You look worried.'

'It's hardly surprising after what we've just been through, is it, Izzy?'

'No, not at all. So what have you been thinking, Ted?'

'I think it's best that you and Robert go back to Nairobi for a while where you'll be a lot safer than here at Kingston Farm.'

'But what about you, Ted? How will you cope out here, all by yourself?'

'Don't worry about me, Izzy. I've got Juma, Elena and the dogs for security and company.'

'Okay, if that's what you think is best, but Robert and I will miss you terribly, won't we, Bobby?' Izzy said as she rolled the big rubber ball back in his direction.

'And that reminds me, Izzy, do you remember what we discussed on our way back from the Victoria Hotel, Nairobi, in October?'

'Do you mean my idea of starting up a dress-making business?'

'Yes, you remember "*La Coquette*"?'

'Of course, I do, Ted. That would be a wonderful chance of giving my business idea a go, wouldn't it?'

'I agree, absolutely.'

'Thanks so much, Ted, I really look forward to this opportunity.'

'You're welcome, Izzy,' I say as I bend down to give her an affectionate hug.

I walk slowly upstairs to the study and sit in front of my typewriter, making sure it has enough black ribbon in place and I begin typing my first order of dress fabric for Izzy's new business, "*La Coquette*".

Messrs. A. C. Barbier & Co.,
Box No. 5660
Nairobi
Kenya Colony
British East Africa

Dear Sirs,
I should be grateful if you would send me a catalogue of your fabrics and dress-making materials, specifying the cost in shillings per yard. In addition, if you would consider sending me samples of a selection of your dress-making fabrics, I should be much obliged to you.
Please reply to this letter at the following address:
Messrs. "La Coquette"
Box No. 182, NAIROBI.

Sincerely,
Judge Edward Stephens
Nyeri District, Kenya Colony.

As I sign the airmail letter and add a Tanganyika 20cent stamp, I smile to myself with the knowledge that this is the first piece of private enterprise I have engaged in, and it is on behalf of my beloved Izzy. 'Let's hope it all works out,' I say to myself.

Chapter Thirty-Eight
The Curse

Finally, the *Mau Mau* "freedom fighters" among the Kikuyu gathered moral support due to the brutality of British security forces and troops, while others among them were devising more secretive and pernicious "cures" for British colonialism.

In a dark, secluded part of the Aberdare Forest, a shaman and six senior chiefs of the Kikuyu tribe were meeting to decide the fate of certain *wazungu* who were involved in oppressing the freedom-fighters and denying *Ithaka na Wiyathi,* Land and Freedom to the people. A ceremony was underway, and everyone present was daubed with ochre and white, and wore effigies and masks of ancestral spirit guides.

The clearing in the forest was barely evident in the rapidly-fading light of the African night, and a smell of burning sage was in the air. First, one of the senior chiefs addressed the grizzled shaman dressed in a leopard skin and mask at the centre of the gathering.

'*Mzee na ku-waza,* I think we need something better than spears, *pangas,* fire and brave warriors to drive these *wazungu* away.'

'*Gani,* what were you thinking of, *rafikiangu?*' The shaman asked with a wry smile.

'*Na ku-waza,* I think we need *Gethathi,* powerful curse to stop the *Bwana* judge and his *askaris,*' replied the chief.

Another chief spoke out, 'Will you perform a ceremony with us tonight, *Mzee?*'

'*Ndio kabisa,* yes,' replied the shaman.

'*Wa-patana, wa-patana,* we agree,' the chiefs chanted in unison.

Eyeing the proud cockerel tethered to a stake in the baked earth, the shaman grabbed it by the legs amidst loud squawking and fluttering feathers and began to walk around the gathering, stamping his feet to the sound of a slow, rhythmic *djembe*.

He then began calling on *Ngai na mababu,* God and the ancestral spirits to sanctify the words of the "M*alaika*, spirit" he began to invoke.

When the chanting and dancing had reached a tumultuous pitch, the shaman tore the cockerel's head off with his teeth and sprayed its blood around. After cleansing themselves, the *wazee,* elders then passed a gourd of palm wine around the circle and each drank a libation to the ancestors and spirits invoked this night. The ceremony was complete and the chiefs dispersed without further words being spoken.

Chapter Thirty-Nine
Munthu Hola Detention Camp,
2 January 1954

The arid savannah plain around Hola Detention Camp is slowly illumined with the rapidly growing scourge of the sun's rays. In more distant villages, cockerels' cackling crows joust in the dawning day, and then the faint sounds of humming voices can be heard as fellow prisoners begin to sing the ancient Gikuyu songs celebrating the birth of a new day, and what *Ngai*, the Supreme Spirit, had intended for it.

Finally, the sounds of running water, slop pails, marching feet, banging doors and barked orders begins to slowly pervade the air.

I'm sitting chained in my solitary cell and am trying to focus my mind on my family in Nakuru. I can visualise Wambui preparing the morning *ugali*, and Eliza returning from the river with a bucket of water on her head, while Sam is constructing an impenetrable fort in the sands around our *shamba*. Suddenly, my reverie is shattered when a sliding hatch in the prison cell door is opened, and an order barked.

'Prepare to meet your fate, *Mau Mau* scum.'

The prison guards systematically unlock my manacles and then handcuff my arms behind my back as I'm led out of my disgusting cell, and out into the freshening dawn wind of this new and final day. All of us sense our fate and begin to chant the Gikuyu *Gethathi, Ithaka na Wiyathi,* Land and Freedom, as we are led to a scaffold erected in the middle of the detention camp compound.

Although, there are no witnesses to "*wazungu* injustice" except the guards, *askaris*, and soldiers with rifles, our comrades throughout the camp sense the occasion and a slow rhythmic drumming begins.

It starts with tin plates and mugs being struck against prison bars, and then rhythmically stamping feet and ululations. Soon, a wave of pulsating sound envelops the camp and the soldiers and guards begin to react nervously, removing the safety catches from their rifles and constantly scanning their surroundings.

One by one, my comrades are led up the steps of the scaffold and a black hood is placed over their heads. They are pushed forward to the trapdoor and a lever is pulled sending their bodies downwards and their souls upwards.

My time is here, I now realise, and the wings of my memory fly back to the time of my initiation on the slopes of *Kere Nyaga*, before I became a man. Before we set out on our journey as an "age grade" with my peers, I had been listening to the talk of my older brothers and sisters, and witnessed how that for one moon before the ceremony, they were living in an excited, and sometimes fearful, frenzy.

My brother also told me that as the day approached, he had serious doubts as to whether he had the courage to become a man, but the support of his "age grade", made it possible.

Our day arrived sooner than expected and we were taken off into the forest surrounding Kere Nyaga by my father's brother, Kaka, who performed this important role in our tribe. He had the reputation of being considerate to the boys who followed his instructions, but harsh to those who didn't listen carefully or were boastful.

We were instructed to bring one item on which our survival depended. And this could be anything we chose, from a favourite weapon, a shield, a charm, an item of food, and so on. Because we had a long trek in the forest ahead of us, Kaka advised us it had to be portable and light. I decided to bring my favourite hunting knife which had been a constant companion to me throughout my youth. It was made by our village shaman and iron-monger with a hard wooden handle inlaid with copper wire and a serrated iron blade.

There were ten of us in our "age grade", most of whom I knew very well, and some I avoided because of their boastful natures. I felt that by the time Kaka had finished with us, we would be like a band of brothers. So we set off on our trek soon after we had shared some cassava and mboga, vegetables, which put a spring into my stride as we headed off up Kere Nyaga and the dark forest encircling his generous waist.

The hot sun bid us farewell as we entered the dark canopy of tall trees and lianas that began to shroud the light of day from us. Even now I began to realise that perhaps I should have brought my panga, machete, with me, as some of my peers had sensibly done. Immediately, I noticed that the sounds and smells around me had changed.

I could hear the sounds of macaque monkeys above my head scouring the trees for fruit; and I saw and smelled the spoor of mountain buffalo. As I did so, I said a quick prayer to my ancestors and Ngai, to protect us from a marauding herd.

After some time, and the perspiration had congealed in my hair and eyes, and my arms and legs ached from pushing and hacking through vines and bamboo, Kaka called for us to stop and rest while he asked us some questions about what we had observed on our way here.

'Why is this important, Kaka?' Ndege, my friend, asked.

'Well, if you had to retreat to your first camp, how would you know the way back?'

'Ndio kabisa,' Ndege and others murmured in agreement.

This was the first lesson Kaka taught us and there were many more to follow. Some of my friends had bought cassava roots, plantain, and bananas, which were shared in our hunger. Others had gone off in search of a mountain stream and came back with water in a gourd to share, also.

We were off again after our brief rest, and our pace began to slow a little as the incline of the mountain was becoming steeper, and there were more boulders and fast flowing mountain streams to cope with. But my peers and I pressed on with even greater determination and spirit for we knew that what was to follow would be a greater challenge to our courage and stamina.

We had been trekking higher and higher into the forest belt of Kere Nyaga and I noticed plants I had never seen before, which Kaka told us were giant "lobelias" in which many insect-loving birds lived. Some of these beautiful canaries I had never seen before, nor my peers, and it seemed very magical up here among these strange plants, soils, birds and impenetrable forest mists. It was as if Ngai was slowly unfolding the secrets of his nature to which we had been strangers before.

As the sun became weak in the sky and showed that he would soon sleep, Kaka told us we should make camp and left us to organise the construction of the shelter, hunting for food, the building of the cooking fire and the protection of the camp site. It soon became clear who among us were the most confident leaders of our age grade, and I was proud to be one of them. It was me who

127

took responsibility for collecting leaves and kindling and building the cooking fire using the friction of two sticks and some dry hemp, while Ndege took responsibility for securing our camp site.

As I was organising the kindling, I said to him, 'Are you prepared for the initiation ceremony tonight?'

'Although, my older brother has told me what to expect, Munthu, I still feel anxious that I may lack the courage I will need for becoming a man.'

'Ndio kabisa, surely, I feel the same way, rafikaingu, but I pray to my ancestors that they will give us the strength to endure,' I respond.

So we both throw ourselves into a frenzy of activity in order to forget the trials of tonight. I can sense the tensions in my peers also and realise that we will gain strength and resolution if we can support each other through the impending ritual, which we intend to do.

Once we have eaten our simple meal of mountain hare and cassava, Kaka begins to tell us stories of our tribe going back to the time of "Gikuyu na Moombi" and the nine tribes of the Kikuyu. I feel so proud to come from such an ancient line, which adds to my much-needed resolve for tonight.

Kaka explains that we will need to be away from our village for a week after the initiation ceremony and therefore, tomorrow we need to begin collecting some of the healing mountain herbs to assist in our recovery from the circumcision, which is to be performed tomorrow night by our village shaman.

'Sasa usiku, tonight wa-kijana, you will be visited by mababu, your ancestor spirits and they will have a special message for you, which I want each of you to remember, because the message they bring you will help you face your initiation into our tribe as men.'

With this message seeping into our minds, we went to our shelter made from cut bamboo stems bound with lianas, and covered with palm fronds to keep out the mountain rain. I was one of the last to enter, and said to Ndege, who was the first to stand guard, 'Promise me one thing, Ndege?'

'Gani, rafikiangu, what, my friend?'

'That if our ancestors come for us tonight, we will look out for each other?'

'Ndio kabisa, of course,' Ndege replies reassuringly.

'Ku-kubali, I agree, also.'

We signify our blood brotherhood by each of us cutting our right palms with my hunting knife and holding our hands together tightly, mingling our blood.

None of us can settle this night, and our shared fears are not allayed by the arrival of a mountain storm which punches holes in our shelter and sends bolts of Ngai's fire streaming through the night sky, making it impossible for any of us to sleep. And just when we felt matters could not become worse, there are terrible shrieking sounds all around us and we each decide to take our chances on the mountainside. I am the last to leave our shelter and grab my special hunting knife for protection before I go.

There is complete confusion all around me as I witness, in between Ngai's flashes of anger, my peers running hither and thither crying out and being pursued by men wearing terrifying masks and wielding sticks with which they are striking us. In my haste to escape, I forget Ndege, and feel already that I have betrayed his trust and our pact of mutual support.

What a feeble and unreliable friend I have turned out to be, I chastise myself. All around me, I hear the fearful cries of my peers running to escape the wrath of their ancestors. Some run back the way we came, while others look for holes or tree trunks to hide in. In the end, I cannot escape, and my ancestor finds me wedged into the fork of an inyenge tree. He stands at the base of the tree with his baleful eyes piercing me like arrows, and a horrible sound finds its way from his throat, like a curse.

'Kijana dhaifu, weak boy! Why are you cowering from your babu, ancestor? I have a message for you.'

I can hardly speak and make myself heard above the wild wind, crashing thunder and lashing rain, but I stutter, 'Gani Mzee, what is it, Sir?'

'Kijana, Munthu, you have been chosen to protect your peoples' ancestral lands. To keep them safe from the kiengere na wazungu, the pink frogs, the British, who would steal it from us.'

Before I can help myself, I say, 'Ni kusudia, I will, Mzee.'

As I utter these fateful words, I have a feeling that they have a portent which I cannot understand, and the mask that bore babu, the spirit of my ancestor, has already melted away in the dark.

Now it's my turn, I say to myself, as I'm led up the steps. I shall hold myself in strength and courage, as *ma-babu,* my spirit ancestors, have always encouraged me to do. I pray to *Ngai* for the safety and welfare of Wambui, Eliza and Sam, and for *Ithaka na Wiyathi*, Land and Freedom, for my tribe.

A fleeting image of Wambui, Eliza and Sam come into my mind's eye as the black hood is placed over my head. It's of their last celebratory homecoming in the village, and Sam and Eliza are sitting either side of Wambui, eating, while Bado and I exchange glances of gratitude. And then I'm falling, and falling towards the snows of *Kere Nyandarwa, Ngai na mababu,* God and my ancestors.

The hangman's voice shouts down to his colleague below, 'Right, Jack. Cut him down, chuck him in the trolley with the others, and that will be our lot for the lime pit this morning.'

'Right you are, Steve. A good morning's work, I reckon, don't you.'

'Perfect job, mate,' Steve, the hangman, concludes.

That same night, there is a terrible thunderstorm and all the inmates of Hola Camp and the surrounding villages say to themselves: *Ngai ekenogora egithie komemenda na koingata tho ciayo,* which means that *Ngai* has cracked his joints in readiness to go to smash and chase away his enemies.

They are all agreed that this is a good sign and a promise that one day soon, *Ithaka na Wiyathi*, Land and Freedom, will be ours.

Chapter Forty
Karibu, Bwana Henry Kingston Farm, Nyeri, 5 February 1954

Back at Kingston Farm, the night of Isabel's confinement comes quickly, and she is lying lady-like among a large pile of silk cushions. Her auburn hair is spread about her pillows framing her high forehead and blue eyes and patches of perspiration are gathering in her night gown as she flicks her right, elegant wrist, which is holding her tortoiseshell fan. Meanwhile, Elena is making a grand fuss of her.

'Elena, pass me the pile of towels *tafadhali.*'

'*Ndio*, yes, *Memsab.*'

'*Haya,* here, *Memsab,*' Elena says, placing a bundle of clean white towels to my right side.

'*Asante sana*, Elena.'

'*Hata kidogo,* you're welcome,' she replies.

There's a firm knocking on the door.

'*Nani,* who is it?'

'It's Juma, *Memsab.*'

'*Karibu* na *kuja hapa,* welcome and come in, Juma.'

Juma carefully opens the bedroom door and hands Elena a large copper pitcher of hot water. Elena moves towards the large tin bath at the end of Isabel's bed and gently pours the hot water into it. The steam rises to the ceiling and momentarily conceals a squadron of mosquitos hovering by the kerosene lamp overhead.

'*Asante sana*, thank you, Juma.'

'*Hata kidogo,* you're welcome, *Memsab.*'

After Juma closes the bedroom door with a big smile from Elena, Isabel motions Elena to sit at the end of her bed.

'Elena, now *Bwana* Edward is happy about my new baby, I pray it will make things better between us.'

'*Kweli,* surely, *Memsab,*' Elena responds smiling.

Henry arrives at two in the morning, his crowning head being celebrated with whoops of joy by Elena, who acts as midwife on this occasion.

'*Kichwa ekundu,* red head, *Memsab. Masai kidogo,* little Masai,' says Elena.

In among a series of rapid breaths, and determined pushing, Isabel utters, 'Yes…you're…right…Elena. He's a little…red…and…white…*Masai.*'

'Push, *Memsab*…Push. *Bwana kidogo kuja,* the little man will be here very soon. *Kuja sasa.*'

'Here…goes…Elena…One…last…push.'

Elena gently grasps and supports the crowning head of the minuscule Masai warrior, Henry, while Isabel takes a deep breath and pushes with all her remaining strength. Suddenly, a red-pink blur of glistening flesh, bone and sinewy tissues springs out, fully formed and screaming. The writhing, crying mass that is Henry is greeted with tears and cheers and, for once, Edward is home.

'*Memsab*, a boy! I get *Bwana* Edward.'

'Do, Elena,' Isabel says with deep tiredness, relief and joy.

After washing Henry and rubbing me with the hot towels, Elena leaves Isabel to suckle my new boy, who is red, sore and disconsolate after a swift labour and sudden birth.

'*Masai kidogo,*' the little red-haired warrior latches on to Isabel's breast, holding on with great determination, after a few unsuccessful attempts.

'Thank God, you're here, Henry,' Isabel sighs contentedly.

Soon, Edward comes into the bedroom with joyous strides.

'How wonderful that Henry's here. Congratulations, my darling Izzy,' Ted says, kneeling beside me and stroking my face gently. He then turns his attention to Henry, who is suckling at the breast, and kisses the top of his reddish head.

'It was incredible, Ted. It was all over in an hour of pushing and encouraging cheering from Elena.'

Elena bursts into peals of laughter, and Edward smiles a rare, beaming, sunny smile. His parents would be proud of them now that they have two heirs to the Stephens' name. The "Law of Necessity" that has been the predominant ruler of Edward's time in Kenya Colony is briefly abrogated and replaced with feelings of hopeful optimism for a change.

Chapter Forty-One
Taking Control Kingston Farm,
Nyeri, 24 April 1954

A select few of Judge Edward Stephens' colleagues have gathered together for an informal lunchtime meeting to discuss an "action plan" following the British authorities launch of "Operation Anvil" whereby General George Erskine and ten battalions of infantry have been deployed to seal off Nairobi from outside contact and have begun systematically rounding up all members of the Kikuyu, Embu and Meru tribes people with a view to "screening" them for internment and interrogation as *Mau Mau* sympathisers and therefore, potential rebels.

In this manner, over 30,000 "suspects" are interned without trial, all are screened in "the Pipeline", thousands are tortured, and over 1,100 hanged.

Judge Edward Stephens, Chief Inspector Mike Anderson and Charles Wood are sitting around the dining room table relaxing, having eaten a generous chicken curry served by Juma and Elena. After topping up the crystal carafes of whisky and water, the servants have retired to the kitchen, allowing the "Nyeri District triumvirate" to commence their discussion.

'So, Mike, what do you anticipate will be the reaction of the Kikuyu and other tribes to the massed internment, screening and interrogation of their people,' Edward asks.

'Well, so far, the mood seems remarkably quiet, and may be merely a sign of their shock and awe at the audacity of the army and security forces,' Mike replies.

'I would agree with your assessment, Mike, and would add that my informants have told me that because of a tip off beforehand, General China and Dedan Kimathi's forces have almost trebled in size in and around the Aberdare and Mount Kenya forests,' Charles interjects.

'I guessed that might happen,' says Edward, and adds, 'I believe the British forces have anticipated the escalation of the guerrilla war, and are now deploying Lincoln bombers to carpet bomb the insurgents in order to deal with this counter-contingency. Is that right, Mike?'

'You're right on the money there, Ted, and my sources inform me that they have enough bombs and munitions to thoroughly torch the forests so there's nowhere for these terrorists to hide from us.'

'So from where you're sitting, Ted, what do you anticipate will happen around Nyeri District, Rift Valley Province?'

'In all honesty, Charles, I anticipate that oathing ceremonies will multiply exponentially among the Kikuyu, Embu and Meru tribes and that episodes like the "Larri massacre" will become more common,' Ted replies.

'What you're saying, in effect, Ted, is that we have a *de facto* civil war on our hands,' says Charles.

'Precisely,' interjects Mike. 'And as a result of this, I've requested that General Erskine authorises the deployment of at least two battalions of his infantry to secure government and private property throughout Nyeri District, as well as the key infrastructure of the province.'

'Well, let's hope and pray that it all works out for the best, gentleman. This seems to be our final push, and our lives and livelihoods depend on its successful implementation, so let's drink to its success, shall we?' Edward says, finally.

Assenting voices echo Edwards's remark. "Absolutely…Hear, hear. Cheers!"

The "Nyeri District triumvirate" drain their whisky glasses and go on their separate ways.

Chapter Forty-Two
Wazungu Kuiba Kutuaetu na Kuchinja Mwitu The British Steal Our Land and Destroy Our Forests, May 1954

The sounds of massed and heavy vehicular travel can be heard interspersed with gunfire, shouting and screaming, as columns of British army vehicles, infantry and askaris encircle the Kikuyu village outside Nakuru where Wambui, Liza and Sam have their home and *shamba*. Amidst the scenes of women and children being herded into the back of army trucks can be seen youths throwing stones and spears at the troops, who retaliate with live rounds and baton charges.

'*Ayeee, Bwana! Kwa nini,* why are you doing this to us?' Wambui screams at the *Mzungu* officer-in-charge of a large contingent of armed *askaris* confronting her.

'It's for your own protection against the *Mau Mau* terrorists,' replies the officer wielding his pistol.

'*Bwana,* this is a lie! *Wazungu kuiba kutuaetu,* you are stealing our land!' Wambui shouts angrily.

'These are our orders, so I advise you to get in these trucks, or I cannot guarantee your safety,' the officer responds.

'*Bila shaka,* without doubt, you are liars, you *wazungu,* and may *Ngai* and our ancestors curse you and your children for all time,' Wambui says vehemently.

'I don't for a moment believe your black magic, woman. Now, get in the lorry or it will be worse for you,' the officer waves his pistol dismissively.

As he does so, Sam rushes at the officer with both his fists flailing. The officer responds by hitting Sam on the head with his revolver. Wambui and

Eliza scream and go to Sam's defence with arms and fists flailing, but they are driven back by the rifle butts of the *askaris*. The family are herded like cattle into the nearest army lorry, and are driven away amidst escalating sounds of shouting, screaming and weeping.

As the lines of army trucks fill up with their desperate human cargoes, a contingent of *askaris*, backed by infantry, begin herding the cows and goats belonging to the dispossessed Kikuyu. Within an hour, all that is left of village life are signs of half-prepared meals on untended fires, overturned gourds of water and chickens wandering around scavenging *posho*, maize meal, from the overturned cooking pots.

Fire from Heaven

Meanwhile, above these scenes of calculated brutality, a squadron of Lincoln bombers are heading towards the Aberdare and Mount Kenya forests where the inflated forces of General China and Dedan Kimathi have been gathering. Many of their number are desperate fugitives from the British pincer movement around Nairobi, Operation Anvil, as a result of which over 30,000 Kikuyu, Embu and Meru have been interned without trial and await interrogation, torture and death in "the Pipeline".

Those survivors who have escaped Nairobi have found their way to the mountain lairs of the growing number of *Mau Mau* comrades and their courageous leaders. Despite their efforts at cunning camouflage and the discrete dispersal of smoke from their fires, the Royal Air Force, with its squadron of Lincoln bombers, has amassed over a million bombs in order to torch and destroy these recalcitrant rebels living in the forests.

The sounds of a radio crackle at 20,000 feet, and the Lincoln bomber navigator is talking.

'That's it, bombardier, your target is imminent. Receiving me? Over'

'Loud and clear, Jack. Ordnance is loaded and primed for drop. Over.'

'Pilot, here. Coming in for a low-level sweep now. Prepare to drop in 5 seconds, counting. Over.'

'Ready and waiting. Over.'

The radio crackles once again, but the instruction is clear.

'Now! Over and out.'

With that instruction, a payload of 20 tons is unleashed, comprising 100 thousand pound bombs full of TNT.

The effect on the *Mau Mau* comrades below is devastating as whole swathes of the forest; its hardwood trees, bamboo, liana, palms and variegated animal, bird and plant life are engulfed in unquenchable flames, burning, heat and smoke. Those *Mau Mau* who are not obliterated directly, catch fire and burn, or are blown hither and thither like discarded leaves, their bodies, limbs and spirits, irrevocably broken and dispersed.

For a brief moment, the Lincoln bomber's radio crackles into life.

'Well, we all know who will be frying tonight, don't we, chaps?'

The pilot's comment is greeted by satisfied cheers and laughter all around.

The combination of the successful RAF bombing strategy, "Operation Anvil" and the dispossession, internment, interrogation, torture and hanging of *Mau Mau* suspects and terrorists, enabled a triumphant Evelyn Baring, Governor of Kenya Colony, to declare an "Amnesty to all *Mau Mau* activists" on 18 January 1955. As no Kikuyu or other tribes' people came forward, he withdrew the offer in the summer of the same year, much to the satisfaction of the British colonial settlers.

The *Mau Mau* rebellion had been comprehensively defeated by British land and air forces, and the Lincoln bombers flew home. Ndege, Munthu's age grade friend from the days of his initiation was one of the nine hundred victims claimed in the RAF bombardment of the Aberdare and Mount Kenya forest ranges. The metal planes of the RAF bombardment had swiftly ended Ndege's ("bird" in Swahili) precious life in this final aerial assault.

Chapter Forty-Three
Isabel and Edward Kingston Farm,
21 March 1955

There was air of celebration among the Luo and Kikuyu servants last night which was signified by drumming which resonated throughout the house causing Robert and Henry a disturbed night as they woke constantly and asked their parents about the meaning of the *ngoma*, drumming. It was clear by the morning what it had all been in aid of as the short rains had started and the farmers in the fertile Rift Valley were celebrating its arrival.

The three peaks of *Kere Nyaga* were obscured by a veil of dark cloud and mantling mists which seeped into the surrounding rain forest promising plentiful irrigation for the parched *shambas* of the Kikuyu, and water for the Masai herds in the arid savannah of the lower Rift Valley. Edward was the first to wake.

'God, that was a terrible night, wasn't it, Izzy? I couldn't get a wink of sleep between the drums and the kids. Could you, my darling?'

Isabel was still only half conscious as she stirred beside Ted and seemed to have something else on her mind.

'Er…yes, it was awful, Ted, and I'm exhausted, too. But there's something I've been meaning to tell you, Ted,' she said as she turned to face Ted.

'And what's that, my dear.'

'Well…I think I'm pregnant again.'

Edward sits bolt upright in bed.

'You can't be serious, Izzy. We agreed that we weren't going to have any more children, didn't we?'

'Yes, that's true, Ted, but I think my cap wasn't full proof, and…'

'My God! What a disaster!'

Ted's utterance cause Isabel to take a sharp intake of breath, and gather herself to respond.

'Actually, Ted, I don't think it's such a disaster, after all…'

'It's okay for you to lie and say that, but can't you see; this goes against all the plans we've made and agreed for good reasons.'

'I think you're overreacting, Ted, and if…'

'Overreacting! What's the damn point of making plans when you just ignore them?'

'For heaven's sake, Ted, I said it was an accident!'

'What a convenient accident for you, then.'

'God, I resent that, I really do. After all, it's me that bears the burden of the children from start to finish.'

'And who the hell do you think provides for us all?'

'That's it. I'm off. I can't stand your mean and patronising attitudes anymore.'

'Have it your own way'

'I will.'

Isabel

With that parting comment, I promptly get up and go to the bathroom, leaving Ted to fume inwardly. At least he hasn't gone off his head, as he's prone to do, I reflect with some relief. I remember the last time Ted lost his temper; it was when Robert and Henry were playing in the drawing room and they had decided to use one of the Kelims as a "magic carpet" to help propel them from one side of the drawing room to the other.

They were happily doing this, with Cleo and Rex barking and joining in, when Ted came home from the court at lunchtime and saw them. He was furious with them and started to threaten them with his riding whip. I rushed in from the kitchen, grabbed them both and barricaded myself in the bedroom until Ted calmed down and went away. I was terrified for them and me. He's like a bloody volcano when he goes off!

Ted

What's wrong with Izzy? I muse. Why does she behave so irresponsibly? Can't she see that we have enough on our plate already, without another mouth to feed? I briefly recall Isabel's anxiety about having children in Kenya while we were still courting in Dublin. I really don't understand the female psyche; I really don't, I conclude.

Chapter Forty-Four
Bwana Standish is Born Eldoret,
5 September 1955

The view from the district hospital in Eldoret, Rift Valley Province, is a mixture of sweeping light brown savannah grasses interspersed with cedar and clumps of acacia trees, and in the distant background is a conical-shaped mountain which is an extinct volcano, Mount Elgon. All manner of stories have emanated from the slopes of this mountain, where the Elgeyo (Ndorobo) tribe live amidst cave-dwelling elephants populating the foothills and grasslands below.

The creation-myths of the honey-gathering Elgeyo tribe attracted an inquisitive Swiss psychologist, Dr Carl Gustav Jung, who sought to expand on his theory of "individuation" and a renewal of meaning in his life in the autumn of 1925. It is here that *Bwana* Standish is born.

I'm free-floating like an oyster that's lost its shell, drifting amidst murky, slippery saltiness. I'm on my own and waiting reluctantly to be born. Up to now I've been feeling safe and warm held in this mysterious, silky womb. Yet something's happening. I'm being pushed and thrust this way and that, and sense that I'm being propelled into an uncertain world.

However attractive the prospect of being free from this womb space appears, I hesitate. Something in me, and my mother, is hinting of catastrophe. There's a lurking sense of dread, like an irregular beat. So I hang on in here, and no amount of pushing by my mum seems to make a difference. Her waters just get inkier, and my space cramped and distorted in surprising ways.

I feel panicky and breathless, and I notice it's flowing into a darker, more cramped tunnel, and I'm being squeezed in every part of my being. I can't imagine coming to the end of this convoluted tube. I breathe quickly and swallow gobbets of fluid. There are lights in my eyes, and when I stop breathing, they get brighter.

The swallowing increases, and before I'm ready, I'm floundering, splashing and gasping, becoming a slippery pink blob screaming for all I'm worth. Mum picks me up and places me on her tummy where I recover some calming, yet grasping balance. At last I'm born. This is life; let's just get on with it.

What I remember most is staring at this endlessly white ceiling in which there seems to be a rotating blade. The breeze calms me for a while and then it dawns on me: I'm alone. The sense, touch and smell of her presence are gone, and I'm bereft. The waves of convulsing crying are to no avail.

I have a mental picture of long, grey, squat buildings joined by concrete ramps, and men in white coats with snakes around their necks leaning over beds.

'You must take some milk, Master Standish,' I hear a voice say. Although, I feel a gnawing in my guts, the bottle seems a poor substitute for my mother's breast with its reassuring warmth, comfort and taste.

Each night I lie here, waiting for her return, but she never comes. Instead, I have the sporadic visitations of nurses sailing up and down the endless, Dettol-smelling corridors with their fleeting smiles in their starched white linen. I miss her smell, voice and presence with each passing day. This sprawling concrete prison becomes a constantly growing menace and I can't exactly remember when my imprisonment here comes to an end.

The next thing I know, I have arrived at Kingston Farm, but two other boys, older than me, have beaten me to it. They are my brothers, Hen and Bob, and they introduce me to my new home which is a large wooden house with an extensive veranda overhung with beautiful yellow and blue climbing flowers which seem to cool the equatorial sun that constantly shines.

Compared to my former white prison, here there is so much going on, and much of it seems to centre on me, and our two canine friends, Cleo and Rex. Bob spends a lot of his time singing me nursery rhymes, while Hen tempts me into numerous adventures at the farm.

Chapter Forty-Five
Wambui, Eliza and Sam Ku-Kumbuka,
Remembrance, 20 October 1955

It had been three years ago that "the Emergency" had been declared by the colonial authorities, and since then over a million Kikuyu had been forcibly evicted from their ancestral lands, 30,000 interned without trial, many thousands tortured and hanged, but the biggest burden of suffering had fallen on 25,000 innocent children under the age of ten who had died from starvation and malnutrition.

These crimes against humanity and an innocent populace would be hidden from the public view and record for the following sixty years. In the meantime, what remained of the vanquished and broken Kikuyu population had to survive and possibly thrive.

A few Kikuyu clans and families had managed to find their way back from their forced internment in the "fortified villages" to the *shambas* of their ancestors in the area surrounding Nakuru. Among them are Wambui, Eliza and Sam. Wambui's skeletal form seems to have shrunk in size and stature and the limbs of her prematurely-aged; *wakijana,* children, look almost stick-like as they plod back to the overgrown wasteland that is their *shamba na nyumbani,* farm and home.

Their livestock had long since been confiscated by the security forces, consumed or destroyed. What remains of their crops of *mahindi, mboga na maharagwe,* maize, vegetables and beans has, likewise, been obliterated. They will have to begin all over again. Wambui is the first to speak.

'Sam *na* Eliza, *kuja hapa,* come here. I hid some *pangas na jembes,* machetes and hoes from the security forces in case they stole them from us.'

Wambui walks slowly towards what remains of a sacred fig tree, *mikoyo,* and begins digging away the earth with her bare hands. Soon, the children join in and the precious tools are uncovered. Underneath the red earth that conceals the *jembe na panga,* is an iconic reminder of Wambui's former life with Munthu. It is the remaining symbol of his initiation into manhood and the age grade of his tribe: the inlaid hunting knife that he left behind when he was arrested with Bado, beaten and transported to a prison beyond her ken.

Eliza and Sam come to each side of Wambui and hold her like the supporting branches of a family tree and weep. But these are mixed tears of gratitude, sadness and triumph and not of despair. Wambui speaks again.

'*Sasa wanangu,* now my children, let us begin again for *Baba's* sake.'

'*Ndio kabisa,* yes, surely, *Mama,*' her children agree, drying their tears.

While Wambui proceeds to clear away the undergrowth surrounding the area where their huts once stood, Eliza begins searching for any surviving *calabashes* with which to collect water from the nearest stream, and Sam takes on his father's mantle and begins to chop branches from the overgrown acacia trees to begin the reconstruction of their *nyumbani,* home.

After some hours have elapsed, other members of Wambui's tribe find their way to the slowly resurrected homestead of the "Mkesi clan". They appear in ones and twos, young and old bearing gifts of *mahindi, maharagwe na ndizi,* maize, beans and bananas. It is traditional among the Kikuyu to share among themselves what few crops or other supplies that are available so that no one goes without.

This natural generosity helped to sustain the survivors of "the Emergency", the villagisation and its lethal aftermath.

Soon, in the centre of the clearing that Wambui and her daughter have made, a new *nyumbani,* home, begins to take shape, and most important of all, Sam, in his father's role as "fire-maker and keeper", has re-constructed the *"Mkesi moto",* or hearth fire.

As Wambui, Eliza and Sam sit around their hearth and its three stones for cooking with a few other clan members, she prays to *Ngai na mababu,* God and her ancestors, that she might also meet her *mume,* husband, again one day.

Chapter Forty-Six
Isabel Kingston Farm, 1 April 1956

The short rains are coming to an end, once again, and Elena tells me that the Kikuyu tribes' people have been re-constructing their *nyumbani na shambas*, homes and farms after the terrible time they suffered at the hands of the security forces and *askaris*. I still feel ambivalent about all this going on in our Nyeri District.

On the one hand, I felt terribly afraid of another attack from the *Mau Mau* who nearly massacred us and Robert eighteen months ago, and on the other, I can see that they only wanted to protect their ancestral lands and way of life. Stan's screaming again, for heaven's sake. I hope Bob and Hen haven't been bothering him again, or he may be hungry. I'll go and check.

As Isabel leaves her bedroom and goes downstairs to the playroom, she begins to reflect on the course of her life now and how it might have been if she had stayed in London with Francesco. Her thoughts go to the time when she and Francesco were seeing a lot of each other, and had spent the evening together at the Leopard's Club in Soho.

'You are the most wonderful Tango dancer, Francesco,' Isabel says.

'Well, Isabella, you know it takes two to Tango.'

'You cheeky fellow!'

'No, Isabella, I really mean it. You're a natural dancer. Where did you learn?'

'Well, I have to admit to taking a class in ballroom Tango dancing when I was at Rathmines Secretarial College.'

'You certainly learned the technique well, didn't you?'

'Changing the subject, Francesco, do you mind if I ask you something?'

'What's that, dear Isabella?'

'I...I've decided to marry Ted, and...'

'You can't be serious, Isabel, after all that we've talked about.'

'You must understand, Francesco, that I've got to think about my future, and...'

'I can assure you a future here in London, Isabel, if you'll only trust me.'

'It's not that I don't trust you, Francesco, but you're already married, and I have to think about what I want for myself.'

'But Ted's so possessive and controlling and that won't change, Isabella, will it?'

'I'm not sure, Francesco, but I've got to give it a go. It's my one chance.'

'All right, Isabella, it's your life, not mine, and I won't stand in your way, if that's what you want.'

'Thanks, Francesco, I appreciate your understanding.'

'Fine. But let me ask you one thing, Isabella.'

'What's that, Francesco?'

'Why didn't you tell me about this plan of yours before?'

'I didn't want to spoil our time together, Francesco, but I knew the time had arrived.'

'I just wish you had been clear with me, that's all, Isabel.'

'I'm sorry, Francesco, but I find it hard to talk about my feelings openly a lot of the time, you know.'

'You do keep your inner life to yourself, don't you, Isabella?'

'I do, indeed, Francesco.'

So the dye was cast, and I arranged for Ted to come over to London. He stayed with his sister, Elizabeth, the night before our wedding at the Oratory Church in Kensington that fine Easter day. Ted was as keen as I was to make it a very small family affair, and he even agreed for Francesco to be our "witness" when signing the register. I still have a picture of him in my wardrobe proudly holding my right arm, smiling and looking like the kind, magnanimous gentleman that he is.

'Elena, *una fanya nini,* what's happening here?' I say to Elena as I view the absolute shambles of the playroom. There is an overturned red tricycle, a makeshift den made from Ted's best Kelim rugs and overturned settees, and Robert and Henry painted as red Indian squaws with my best make-up kit. In

147

the corner of the playroom is a very disconsolate Stan bawling his head off in the pram.

'Do you like our red Indian faces, Mummy?' Robert asks as Henry stands alongside him grinning from ear to ear.

'It's very nice, boys, but what about Stan? Can't you see your noise is upsetting him?'

'Sorry, Mummy,' they chorus.

As I stand there watching the results of the boys' natural exuberance, I have a little more sympathy for Ted and his aversion to noise and chaos.

'*Memsab, watoto wa-cheza,* the boys were only playing.'

'*Nijua,* I know, Elena, but look at poor Stan!'

'*Samahani,* I'm sorry, *Memsab!*'

'*Wasiwasi,* don't worry, Elena, I will just feed Stan to calm him down.'

'*Ndio kabisa,* yes, of course, *Memsab.*'

With that response, I lift Stan out of the cot to give him a feed and a cuddle, and as I do so, I recall with some relief that all the guilt and unease I carried with me until the birth of Henry is now gone. And I now realise that I made the right decision to leave Francesco and marry Ted and come to this beautiful but deeply troubled country.

Chapter Forty-Seven
Bado Kuja Kwetu, Bado Comes Home
Nakuru, May 1956

Life in Wambui's village has almost returned to normal after the terrible sufferings, dislocations, imprisonments and worse that have befallen the Kikuyu tribe since the introduction of "the Emergency" four years ago. Agriculture has more or less returned to normal, livestock has gradually been replaced at great cost and sacrifice, but the terrible memories of suffering and loss remain.

Eliza has taken on some of the tasks her mother used to perform, like fetching firewood and mending clothes, and Sam has become *mwanamume,* the man of the household, which includes caring for the family's newly-acquired herd of goats and some chickens. But they all work together in their *shamba,* weeding, planting and harvesting their *maharagwe, mahindi na mohogo,* beans, maize and cassava.

It is late afternoon in the village, Wambui is pounding *mahindi* in the large wooden pestle, Sam is tending to the goats and Eliza is returning from her long trip to the river where she has been fetching water for the evening meal. Eliza is the first to notice a familiar figure that she hasn't seen since her father, Munthu, was arrested, brutally assaulted and transported to an internment camp a long way from Nakuru.

'*Mama, kuja!* Mum, come! *Haraka!* Hurry! Bado *ni hapa,* he is here!' Eliza cannot contain her feelings, as she puts down the containers of water. Bado approaches her and stands facing the young woman, who was only a girl two years ago.

Before Eliza stirs, Sam has already thrown himself into the outstretched arms of Bado, who lifts the stocky youth off the ground in a heartfelt embrace.

'*Karibu kwetu, rafikiangu. Hujambo*. Welcome home, friend. How are you?' Sam shouts excitedly.

'*Sijambo*, Sam! *Habari ako*, how are you?'

'*Nzuri kabisa*, very well, Bado.'

Meanwhile, Eliza embraces Bado, and Wambui arrives to complete the family reunion.

'*Habari za safari*, how was your journey?' Wambui asks.

'*Safari ndefu*, it was a long journey, *Mama, lakini kwa kwetu*, but I'm home,' Bado replies, grinning broadly. Wambui and Eliza cannot restrain their tears of joy at seeing Bado.

Sam says, '*Kuja nyumbani,* Bado, come to our hut,' taking the hospitable mantle of his father, Munthu.

As the two men walk together in front of Wambui and Eliza, who cannot contain their excitement, Wambui calls after them, '*Kutengeneza kuku na* Bado, *mwanangu,* prepare a chicken for Bado, my son.'

'*Ndio kabisa*, surely, *Mama,*' he replies.

After the chicken has been killed and prepared for cooking by Bado, the women begin cooking the meal of *posho, mboga na kuku*, boiled maize, vegetables and chicken for their honoured guest.

There is little talk as the four of them begin to enjoy the feast that everyone has helped to prepare for Bado. When he is satisfied, he speaks, '*Chakula vizuri sana*, the food is very good, *Mama*,' Bado says, smiling gratefully at Wambui.

'*Karibu sana,* you are very welcome, Bado,' Wambui responds.

She then looks at Bado in an enquiring and somewhat anxious way, and asks, '*Rafikiangu, habari,* how's Munthu?'

There is a heavy silence between them as Bado stares into the cooking fire and prepares to share the sad news.

'*Habari baya,* Wambui, *lakini* Munthu *kwa mababu*. Bad news. I'm sorry to say, Munthu is with the ancestors,' Bado says as he looks at Wambui directly.

'*Hapana, hapana,* no, no,' Wambui says, and starts to sob uncontrollably, clinging to Eliza and Sam for mutual comfort.

'*Pole, pole,* sorry, sorry,' Bado says comfortingly to all three, embracing them with his outstretched arms as they share their grief and sadness with him.

'*Nimeshapoa,* thank you, *rafikiangu,*' she says, slowly trying to regain her composure, and wiping her eyes with her *kitenge,* sari.

'He asked me to send you and the children his love and blessings…'

'*Kweli,* truly, Bado?'

'*Ndio kabisa,* absolutely, Wambui.'

'*Ku-ambia, rafikiangu,* tell me what happened, my friend.'

'*Sikiliza,* listen, Wambui, they tortured him, but he bore it like a man…'

'*Ku-endelea,* continue.'

'The *wazungu* couldn't break his spirit…'

'I am so proud of him, Bado,' Wambui says, looking at Sam.

'He told me about his youth in Nakuru, his *shamba* and how he first met you…'

'How can I forget, *rafikiangu*…'

'*Na sema,* Munthu asked me to look after you all, as his *rafikiangu,* and I will honour that promise now and when the struggle is over. *Ku-ahidi,* I promise.'

'*Sasa, una fanya nini,* Bado? What will you do now?'

'*Sasa,* I will join the fight for *Ithaka na Wiyathi,* Land and Freedom,' Wambui.

'*Lakini vipi,* but how can we win against these ruthless *wazungu*?'

'I believe that *Ngai na mababu,* God and the ancestors, are behind our struggle.'

'*Kweli,* truly, how do you know this?'

'*Kwa sababu,* because on the morning of Munthu's hanging, around mid-day, there was a terrible storm, *na mvua mno,* it rained and rained and thundered, like nothing we had seen before. I knew then that *Ngai* was speaking to us all from *Kere Nyaga.* He was angry at the injustice of his people's loss of their ancestral lands at the hands of the *wazungu*…'

'*Asante sana,* Bado. I now have hope and faith that we will triumph over these ruthless *wazungu,*' Wambui says, finally.

'*Ni-patana,* I agree.'

'*Kabla sijaenda,* before I go, Wambui, I must give you this *Gethiito,* charm. Munthu asked me to return it to you with his love and *Baraka,* blessings,' Bado says.

Wambui opens her hands to receive the cowrie necklace that she gave to her Munthu before he returned to General China, and struggles to withhold her tears as she clasps the charm to her breast.

There is a long pause before Wambui says, *'Wenda wapi, sasa,* where will you go now, *rafikiangu?'*

'I will return to *mwitu Kere Nyaga,* the forest hideout of General China and our *Mau Mau* comrades.'

'May *Ngai na mababu,* God and our ancestors, guide and protect you always. *Safari nzuri, rafikiangu,* safe journey, my friend,'

'Kwaheri na kuona halafu, goodbye, and see you again, Wambui, Eliza *na* Sam.'

As Bado walks away from the village and his new family, he fears in his heart that he may never see them again, but he is determined to continue the struggle for *Ithaka na Wiyathi,* Land and Freedom, no matter what the consequences.

The last thing that Bado sees as he crests the hill overlooking his *kwetu,* new home, is the smoke from the cooking fire and feast that his new family honoured him with on his return from Hola Prison Camp.

Chapter Forty-Eight
Bwana Stan Kingston Farm,
1 September 1958

The aspect I liked most at Kingston Farm was sleeping all together in the same bed and waking up to the incredible views of *Kere Nyaga*, Mount Kenya, where the Kikuyu God, *Ngai*, lived. It was Elena, our maid, who first told me about terrifying *Ngai*, and his anger at the interfering ways of human beings.

Elena had such a sweet face and soft, round form. I loved it when she fed me or bounced me on her knee. She even sneaked me into her hut on her back one day. The Kikuyu *watoto,* children, had never seen a *mzungu*, white, baby on a black woman's back before, so they were greatly amused when I appeared around their hut fire one day. I also loved Elena's sweet, acrid smell, and the gentleness of her touch which was permeated with wood smoke, like her milk.

'*Kuja, Bwana kidogo*, suck up,' she would often say. Of course, it was such a satisfying pleasure and I would suckle for all I was worth some days. With Elena, I was never hungry or bored. One day, Elena took Bob, Hen and I to visit her mother, *Mama mzee,* who lived in a Kikuyu village not far away from Kingston Farm.

I'll always remember our first meal with Elena in her mother's hut, *nyumbani.* The hut was filled with smoke as Bob, Hen and I went inside, and after our eyes got used to the dim light, we found a spot to settle down. In the centre of the hut was a charcoal fire, and suspended over it was a large blackened pot, with a thick white mass boiling away inside it.

'*Watoto wanapenda chakula*, would you like some food, children?' She said.

'*Ndio, Mama Mzee,*' the three of us chorused.

Then *Mama mzee* reached over with a long stick and hooked it onto the pot, and with an amazingly deft movement, she lifted it off the fire and put it to her side.

'*Kuona watoto,* look!' I saw Elena smile as Bob watched her take a handful of the white maize paste and begin moulding it into a ball.

'You see, *Bwana Bob*, do it like this!'

Bob looked a little puzzled but followed suit at the first opportunity. He dropped the *posho* ball on the floor of the hut and howled with pain as he blew on his hand frantically.

'*Pole rafikiangu*, your hands are as soft as a baby's.'

It puzzled me that the villagers could live on such simple food, especially when I thought of our chicken, eggs, sausages and bacon. Nevertheless, they seemed content and mostly happy from what I could see.

After we had eaten our *posho na mboga*, maize and vegetables, *Mama mzee* would give each of us a small gourd of boiled milk which had a sweet, smoky taste, like Elena's milk.

The Mill of Fate

Our most exciting adventure at Kingston Farm began one morning as the cock crowed, even before the sun's rays had peeped above the forests of *Kere Nyaga*.

Hen called out, Stan! Bob! Quick, let's get up and go!'

We stirred reluctantly from our sleep.

'Is it time to get up already?' I said.

'Yes, Stan, look at *Kere Nyaga!'*

We peered, bleary-eyed, at the growing light, and slowly began climbing into yesterday's tee shirts and shorts, and putting on our sandals. As we slid down the wooden staircase, we were rehearsing our plans for the expedition we had planned. Stepping outside the back door, I noticed the sun was climbing into the sky, and I felt excited by the smell of wood smoke, and the sounds of breakfast being prepared in the servants' quarters.

The taste of adventure had been savoured, but just as we thought we had a clear run to our destination, Juma's voice called out, '*Wenda wapi, watoto, where are you going, children?'*

The three of us stopped in our tracks, and whispered to each other conspiratorially. Bob was the first to speak.

'We're going to the Mill, Juma, but please don't tell anyone!'

'This I cannot promise, *Bwana* Bob, *lakini, safari njema,* but go well.'

With that blessing, we were off like a shot, weaving our way along a sandy, scrub-covered, windy path. On our way we encountered Kikuyu mothers and daughters going to fetch water with great big tin drums on their heads. We were amazed that they could carry such terrible weights, and with such seeming elegance, too.

Within a short while of alternatively running and walking, the three of us stood in front of the Mill. Bob, being the oldest, volunteered to stand guard, while Hen and I headed for the quickest way up on to the Mill. Hen and I had agreed that our mission was that of "chief explorers"—like Livingston and Stanley—with a brief to climb the highest building on the horizon. Hen had chosen the particular task of repairing holes in the slate roof.

Getting to the top was the first challenge, which we met by climbing up the vine-covered exterior of the Mill. As we climbed, my heart flew into my mouth as chunks of debris, dust, twigs, leaves drifted into my face. Dodging and spluttering my way up, I noticed a small red-brown scorpion next to my right hand grip. I began trembling uncontrollably and only managed to hold my nerve by changing my route of ascent.

Eventually, Hen and I reached our objective and celebrated our ascent with a banana each from our rations. We both looked down at Bob's diminutive figure which blended in with the surrounding native village with its brown and dusty hues. As we waved to him below, we could hear the sounds and sights of village boys chasing each other with bows and arrows in their pretend battle. Living in Africa was proving to be a great adventure indeed.

As agreed, Hen moved ahead and began removing loose shingles from around the slate roof. I followed behind him cautiously. Within a short time, Hen was surrounded by a sea of slowly shifting slates which seemed to be receding downwards at an alarming rate.

'Hen!' I shouted desperately. He let out an almighty scream and went hurtling downwards and disappeared from my view. Momentarily, I sat on the edge of the abyss, stunned into disbelieving shock. All I could hear and see looking down into the black chasm was an inky, eerie silence. I started to cry despairingly. Finally, I came to my senses, and shouted down to Bob in between my convulsive sobs.

'He's dead!' I shouted down.

'Who's dead?' Bob shouted back.

'Henry's dead!' I shouted back.

Within a trice, I was scrambling down the ivy-clad Mill and planting my feet on the sandy soil.

'Stay here, Bob, while I run and get some help!'

'Sure, quick as you can,' he said, and I ran off as fast as my legs would carry me.

I burst into the kitchen at Kingston Farm, breathless, and shouted, '*Bwana* Henry's dead!'

At first, there was a stunned silence and then Juma and Elena approached me. Juma knelt down in front of me and held my convulsing shoulders with his big hands.

'*Una fanya nini*, what is happening, *Bwana* Stan?'

I spluttered my incoherent reply, '*Haraka, Juma, Bwana* Henry *nataka kufa*, he's dying inside the Mill. Help us! *Tafadhali! Haraka!* Please! Hurry!'

'*Ndio kabisa*, yes, of course, *Bwana Stan. Tuende*! Let's go!'

The three of us made an improbable and incongruous sight as we raced helter-skelter; all the way to the "Mill of Fate". Soon we had a snake-like following of *watoto* from the nearby Kikuyu village, armed with their bows, arrows and spears.

When we arrived at the Mill, Bob was standing with his face next to the cracked Mill door shouting for Hen in ever desperate tones. Sadly, no response greeted his cries. Without a moment's hesitation, Juma had obtained an axe from one of the local village men and began smashing down the rotten Mill door. A great cry of relief went up when the door was finally demolished and the village men poured in. They carried him out on a pallet, more dead than alive and placed him on a blanket on top of the rusty sand outside the Mill.

As his limp and bloodied body lay there inert, patches of blue began to form all over his exposed flesh. I don't remember another thing.

When I woke up later in Kingston Farm in my cotton cocoon, Elena was looking at me anxiously, when I stirred, and said that *Bwana* doctor had been and we had been given some pills to help calm us down.

'*Wapi Bwana* Henry, Elena?' I said drowsily. At that moment, Mum came into the bedroom and I cried with guilt and relief.

'How is he, Mum?' I asked anxiously.

'Don't worry, Stan. Hen's in hospital in Nairobi.'

'Thank God,' I said to myself, and breathed a huge sigh of relief.

I sat up in bed and said, 'I'm very sorry, Mummy, it's all my fault!' I cried.

'Don't worry, my darling, I'm sure it's not all your fault, and we'll find out what really happened, later. Get some more rest, Stan, please.'

I breathed a great sigh of relief as I reflected that I may not carry the entire blame for Hen's death. In my heart, however, I knew that "Judgement Day" would soon follow, whatever promises my dear mother would make me.

Chapter Forty-Nine
Reckoning Edward and Isabel
8 September 1958

Edward is in the living room at Kingston Farm with his back to the French doors which yield a view of Mount Kenya in the rapidly disappearing pink light of an African dusk accompanied by the sounds of tree frogs and a growing crescendo of cicadas. He is holding a glass of whiskey which is half full and addressing Isabel who is sitting opposite him holding a glass of sherry in her left hand, and a physician's report in her right.

'Dr Williams says here that Hen suffered "severe concussion and bruising to the frontal and orbital bones, a broken right scapula and crush injuries to the upper right arm and right pelvis",' Izzy says.

'Basically, Izzy, it's a damn miracle that he's alive, let's be honest. But what I want to know is how this bloody near tragedy came about?'

'Well, Juma and Elena tell me that Bob, Hen and Stan had sneaked out just after dawn last Saturday, and had planned the whole thing beforehand,' Isabel replies.

'What's the point of employing staff is they don't do what they're supposed to?'

'Quite. I have reprimanded them both and said this total lack of care can never happen again.'

'And what was their response, Izzy?'

'They were both very contrite, believe me, Ted.'

'I should bloody well hope so. And what does Dr Williams say? What is Hen's prognosis, Izzy? Has he suffered a brain injury of any sort?'

'Thankfully not. I spoke to him on the phone last night after Hen had regained consciousness. He is covered in plaster from head to toe, but said not to worry and that he will pull through okay.'

'Whatever that means,' Ted interjects.

'Precisely,' Isabel responds.

'But this whole episode brings to mind a topic which I know you're not partial to, Izzy.'

'And what's that?'

'You know; the future education of the boys in England.'

'Do we really have to discuss this now, Ted? Haven't we had enough upset this week to last a lifetime?'

'I don't think avoidance of the subject is a rational approach, personally.'

'My God! You and your "rationality"! Where are your feelings, for heaven's sake, Ted?'

'Don't get so emotional, Izzy. It's time we came to a decision about this matter before we have three totally wild and uncontrollable boys on our hands.'

'Is that what you really think? And what do you propose then, Ted?'

'I propose that we send them to a good boarding school that caters for service families, that's all.'

'That's all. And when do you think's the right time for all this, Ted?'

'Well, after this week's trauma, I would say sooner than later.'

'Christ, Ted! They're so young and innocent! I think it's too soon.'

'Do you want a repetition of this week?'

'Of course not!'

'So grasp the nettle, Izzy, and face the facts. It will be for their own good in the long term, believe me.'

'I don't believe it, Ted. I really don't.'

With that final response, Isabel stands up and leaves her drink and the medical report on the side table as she walks out of the living room. As Edward stands rooted to the spot holding his tumbler of whiskey, he begins to reflect on the exchange with Isabel.

Edward

Why is it that Izzy always flies off the handle when I make a perfectly rational suggestion? Can't she just accept that the boys' education needs to start as soon as possible, before they take on the primitive manners and ways of their black playmates? They're even beginning to speak and behave like them, for Heaven's sake. After all, if she had been a little more cautious in her family planning in the first place, we would only have to consider the education of two of them rather than three, wouldn't we?

Isabel has retreated to the marital bedroom to contemplate Edward's words.

Isabel

It seems to me that Ted resents the children's presence in our lives as an unwanted intrusion. I bet he would be glad to be rid of them so we could enjoy the barren "cocktail high life" of these superficial colonials with too much time on their hands and a total lack of creativity between them. The boys love it here, now that the threat of *Mau Mau* has gone, and I like the fact that they can speak Swahili and relate to the staff as well as their interesting play mates.

This is an exotic adventure playground for them, not without its risks, of course, but they will always remember and treasure these memories when they're grown, I'm sure. If push comes to shove, I know what I'll do: I'll take the boys home to Rathmines, Dublin, as Ma and Da and my sisters have yet to meet them. That's what I'll do, whatever Ted says to try and dissuade me.

Chapter Fifty
Mbare wa Walaika, Family of Angels
Kingston Farm, 14 September 1958

Retribution followed, as night follows day, and Bob and I were grounded for the following week. During that fraught time, we often talked about that expedition to the "Mill of Fate". Dad was furious with rage and took the horse whip to us. Thankfully, Mum's quick intervention and Celtic courage saved our backsides for another day. Eventually, we were forgiven our crimes and Juma was instructed to keep a better watch over us in future. I remember a conversation that I had with Bob at the time.

'What if Hen dies?' I asked.

'I can't imagine it happening.'

'But what if he does, I mean.'

'That's too terrible to think about.

'So what shall we do?'

'What do you mean?'

'I mean about keeping Hen alive.'

'What can we do?'

'I'm going to talk to Juma and Elena, and ask if they can give us some magic medicine to keep Hen alive,' I concluded.

'That's a good idea,' agreed Bob.

So I was delegated to getting hold of some healing herbs or charms that would keep Hen with us at Kingston Farm. I waited till the next day when I began the execution of our plan. I woke early so that I could talk to Juma in the kitchen before the round of daily activities began. When I met him next the kitchen entrance, he was bringing in the firewood for our stove.

'Habara za asabui, good morning, Juma!'

'Habari za asabui, Bwana Stan.'

'Juma, may I ask you a favour?'

'*Ndio,* yes, *Bwana* Stan.'

'I need some herbs or charms.'

'*Kwa nini,* why, *Bwana* Stan?'

'To keep *Bwana* Hen with us,' I replied.

'*Kweli,* truly, *Bwana*?'

'*Kweli*, truly, I'm worried that he may not come back home from Nairobi Hospital.'

'So what kind of charms or magic are you seeking?'

'Something that will heal him, Juma, *tafadhali,* please.'

'*Na sema, Bwana* Stan, tell me, *kwa Bwana* Henry, *napenda zaidi,* what does he most love?'

I immediately thought Mum, but hesitated, as there was someone else that Hen loved most.

'*Bwana* Henry *napenda* Cleo *na* Rex,' I replied.

'*Ndio, Bwana* Stan. *Ndio kabisa,*' he nodded his head vigorously.

With that emphatic response, Juma placed the logs by the kitchen stove and approached me, kneeling down to face me.

'*Bwana Stan*, I have an idea.'

'*Gani*, what kind, Juma?' I asked.

'*Leo tuenda Mondo Mogo*, today I will go to the medicine man and ask him to make this *Gethiito,* charm, for *Bwana* Henry.'

'*Asante sana*, Juma,' I said with huge relief in my voice. I knew at that moment that Juma could help us and that he could obtain just the right charm or medicine for Hen and my heart began to lift for the first time.

A few days and sleepless nights later, I met Juma in the kitchen and asked him if the *Mondo Mogo* had prepared the right charms for Hen. Juma regarded me with a serious and studied look, and beckoned me to come with him, which I did.

The path behind Kingston Farm led, in a roundabout way, to the *Mondo Mogo's* hut. As a *mzungu mtoto*, white European child, I was not allowed into the *mzee's* hut. So I waited patiently while Juma conferred with the *Mondo Mogo*. After what seemed like an eternity of time, Juma emerged with a broad smile and carrying a small parcel, wrapped in leaves.

'*Mzee* asked me to give you this, *Bwana* Stan.'

'*Asante sana*, Juma. Please thank the *Mondo Mogo* for me.'

'Ndio, kabisa, surely, *Bwana* Stan. I will.'

My heart was pounding with joy as I ran all the way back to Kingston Farm carrying the deftly wrapped package in my right hand. That evening, under the cover of darkness, Bob and I opened our magic package which was the gift of the *Mondo Mogu.*

'Can you guess what's inside it, Bob?' I asked excitedly.

'I've no idea,' he replied.

Together, we began to tease out our mysterious, leaf-clad parcel. When we unwrapped it, we found two carved wooden dogs, whittled out of a black, hard wood.

'Aren't they amazing?' I said to Bob as I held one out.

'They're so real, aren't they?' He replied.

As we studied them together, I noticed that the effigies had fat tummies and short, thin legs. And one of them was smaller than the other, like Cleo and Rex. We hugged each other with relief at the arrival of this Kikuyu *Gethiito,* magic from which we had great hopes.

'So how do you think it works?' Bob asked me.

'I think it works by the magic carried in the dogs,' I replied.

'Hmm, I see,' said Bob, as we smiled at each other conspiratorially.

Fortunately, the next day, we were due to visit Hen in Nairobi Hospital, and we decided to secrete the charmed dogs on our person. Bob carried Rex, as he was the oldest, and I carried Cleo, as the youngest. Going back to Nairobi Hospital temporarily brought back all my horrible memories of being abandoned in Eldoret Hospital, so our new environment took some getting used to.

When we eventually got to Hen's bedside, he was covered head to toe in bandages and there were all these octopus-like tentacles hanging down into his arms, like they were feeding on him. And the smell of iodine and surgical spirit made me feel very sick, too. After a long and worrisome interval, Hen eventually stirred and was able to say a few words through his bruised face and broken teeth.

'It's good to see you, Bob and Stan,' he said very quietly.

After Dad and Mum had given Hen a hug, Bob and I positioned ourselves either side of his bed, and put our hands on his. Hen continued, 'How's everyone at Kingston Farm?' He asked almost inaudibly.

'Everyone's fine,' Bob replied.

'What about Cleo and Rex?' Hen asked.

Instead of answering his question, both Bob and I placed our left hands on Hen's bed. Bob said, 'We've got something for you, Hen.'

'What's that?' He asked.

'We've brought magic from the *Mondo Mogo*', I said.

Bob and I simultaneously opened our left hands and the two wooden dogs fell out on to his white sheet.

'Amazing!' Hen said, as he carefully handled and scrutinised each healing dog charm with awe.

We knew, there and then, like Hen, that the magic dogs would bring him home to Kingston Farm. I could almost imagine Hen running his hands down Cleo and Rex's hairy spines, breathing in their doggy smell, and whispering secrets in their attentive but discrete ears.

A couple of weeks later, Hen was sitting on his bed at Kingston Farm, and we asked him what had happened after we had given him the *Mondo Mogo's* magic charms.

'Well, it all happened very quickly,' he began. 'One moment I could hardly lift myself off my pillow, and the next I was walking down the hospital corridor to the lavatory on my own. It was the smell of the bed pans that finally drove me to it,' he joked.

We all laughed out loud at Hen's good fortune.

'So tell us what happened after that?' Bob asked.

'Well, one night while I was lying in my bed trying to sleep, an angel came to the end of my bed. He was very tall and dressed in a bluish-white light robe. At first, I thought I must have been dreaming, and then, as I waited, I'm sure he spoke to me.'

'What did he say?' I asked eagerly.

'He said I had a choice,' Hen replied.

'What kind of choice?' Bob asked.

'He said, I want you to decide whether you want to come with me, or stay with your family and dogs at Kingston Farm,' Hen replied.

'Crickey!' Bob and I chorused.

'Who do you think he was?' Bob asked.

Hen hesitated a little, before he replied, 'He was my Guardian Angel.'

'My God!' Bob and I said.

'So what made you to stay?' Bob asked.

'It was Cleo and Rex, and…you, too,' Hen replied.

'You mean it was the magic dogs that brought you back?' I added.

'Yes,' Hen said emphatically, and we gave each other our triumvirate group hug on Hen's bed.

When I saw Juma again, he was standing upright, with a huge sack of *mahindi,* maize, at his feet in the kitchen.

'Juma! You won't believe it!'

'*Gani,* what, *Bwana* Stan?'

'*Bwana* Hen *kuja kwetu,* he's coming home!'

'*Vizuri sana,* very good, *Bwana* Stan.'

'*Asante sana na Gethiito,* Juma, thank you for your healing charms.'

'*Hata kidogo,* you are welcome, *Bwana* Stan.'

'Juma, *tafadhali,* please tell me how your Kikuyu *Gethiito,* magic works?' I asked.

'*Ndio,* yes, *Bwana* Stan. It was the *Mbare ya Malaika*, the family of angels who helped *Bwana* Henry,' Juma replied.

'Hen said it was his Guardian Angel that came to him.'

'*Ndio,* yes, *Bwana* Stan. It was the Chief of the Angels, working with the spirits of *Bwana* Henry's favourite dogs.'

'So do all spirits, animal and human, work with *Mbare ya Malaika*?'

'*Ndio,* yes, *Bwana* Stan, and remember that *Ngai,* God, is Chief of the *Mbare ya Malaika,* Family of Angels,' Juma said emphatically.

After this event, I regarded Juma with even greater awe than before, and returned to our bedroom to contemplate this deepening mystery of life and spirit. Fortunately, the three of us would not have to invoke *Mbare ya Malaika* for quite some time. The adventure of the Mill had proved too costly in terms of life and limb.

Chapter Fifty-One
Isabel If Only Vogue Could See Me Now
Kingston Farm, 1 December 1958

I'm sitting here in our front garden on a smashing sunny afternoon, and I'm wondering to myself: If only *Vogue* magazine could see me now. I used to be one of their best hat models, and here am I in a somewhat threadbare summer frock seeing that no harm comes to my three wee boys. Robert's over by the rose bed looking to torment insects; Hen's playing with his trucks and Stan is away with the fairies, enacting some play or other.

For the first time in a long while, I feel absolutely safe in this extraordinary land of mountains, forests and savannah plains, and Kingston Farm feels like a proper home. Of course, I do miss Ma, Da and my sisters in Rathmines, but Ted and I have created a family of our own. It's both strange and amusing that the boys speak Swahili as well as their mother tongue. I'm sure the fact that they speak Swahili rather than Gaelic would make Da laugh out loud.

Also I know the boys really feel at home here, and they have made lots of close friends with the Kikuyu boys, especially Eliud's son, Joseph. I still vividly recall the day when Robert, Hen, Joseph and Stan came back to tell me about this lethal rolling machine they had fashioned from an animal feed bin and rolled it from the top to the bottom of a hill. I had visions of Hen's near death experience at the Mill, but they only came back with the usual cluster of grazes, cuts and bruises, thank God.

There was also the day when Hen, Robert and Joseph returned from the farm pond with jam jars filled with tadpoles and jiggers in their feet from walking barefoot among the cow pats. As always, Stan had his head in the clouds and straggled in a long time after the others, also limping from the same. They all seem to have their peculiar, lovable quirks, God Bless them!

It took me and Elena an absolute age to get those wretched parasites out of their feet and they spent the rest of the evening soaking them in soda crystal water. I don't think they'll ever learn!

Cleo and Rex are great with the boys and they're forever rolling in the sand and long grass playing explorers or hunters with our tennis rackets and old bits of sisal rope and sacking. The native boys are even showing them how to make proper spears, bows and arrows, and take them on mock hunting expeditions, which excites their imaginations no end. Fortunately, as yet, they've not killed any game.

I'm feeling tired and a little weak and queasy these days, so I'll take myself off for a siesta so that I'm fresh to attend to preparations for dinner and Ted, when he gets back from the law courts this evening. Also I've got to talk to Ted about my plans to travel to Dublin with the boys before Christmas. I better summon the boys.

'Robert, Hen, Stan! Come on now! It's time for your siesta before Dad comes home!'

Isabel's summons is met with a whelter of protestations, but reluctantly the three boys are marshalled and forced upstairs to their siesta before they can get up to any last-minute mischief for which a dear price will have to be paid when their father returns from work just before dark.

Chapter Fifty-Two
Robert, Hen, Joseph and Stan What is the Point of Thorn Bushes?

It was some weeks before we planned our next adventure, which was to include our *rafikiangu*, Joseph, Eliud's son. One morning, as we were playing hide and seek on the farm, Joseph said he wanted to introduce us to his uncle, Hamid, who had a big *shamba* in one of the nearby villages.

When Joseph talked about Hamid, in my youthful eyes he conjured up an elder, or *mzee,* cultured in one of the many mysterious Kikuyu arts.

Hen and Bob were excited, too, as we rendezvoused at the gate exiting Kingston Farm. After his last reprimand by *Bwana* judge, Juma's discretion barely permitted him to overlook our departure that stunningly bright and glorious January morning. In spite of the growing heat of the day, there was still a vague memory of this morning's crisp dawn overlooked by the snows of *Kere Nyaga.*

Joseph was turned out in his best white shirt and ironed shorts, while Bob, Hen and I were, once again, wearing yesterday's expedition gear.

We set off in single file, with Joseph leading, and followed by Bob, Hen and I, in order of age. As soon as we were out of sight of Kingston Farm, we began to run and walk, in turns, in order to cover more ground, and before we were subdued by the heat of the day. I was always a little fearful of losing my way in the Bush, but one of the many things that impressed me about Joseph was that he weaved his way to his destination like a gazelle.

It was as if he had some kind of inner compass, or eye, which never let him down. He loped across the long, brown, erect stalks of the savannah, while we waded more modestly in his wake.

'So tell me about your Uncle Hamid,' Bob asked Joseph.

'He's my oldest uncle, by my father's side,' replied Joseph.

'Why are you so fond of him?' Hen asked.

'Well, he has always told us good stories from his *safari ndefu*', replied Joseph.

'You mean he was a traveller?' I asked.

'Ndio, Bwana Stan,' he replied.

'Where's he been?' Hen asked, as he skirted a dead tree trunk on our path.

'He told me he went to Lake Kisumu in one evening,' Joseph replied.

'But that's impossible,' Bob said.

'Kwele, Bwana Bob, Uncle Hamid said he had important business to do back home,' Joseph continued. We looked at each other incredulously.

The heat of the day was gaining the upper hand and the pace of *rafikiangu* Joseph had sapped our energy, so we decided to stop under a cluster of thorn trees. We each took huge gulps of our water rations and consumed a banana each. This was turning out to be one of our finest adventures. After refreshing myself, I decided to do a little recce on my own among the large rocks scattered around us.

I was just losing sight of my companions as I poked around in the undergrowth with a stick, when I was overcome by the most searing pain I had ever experienced.

I shouted out and instinctively lifted my left foot into the air and fell against a large boulder. As I examined my foot, I noticed a long thorn sticking out of the sole of my sandal, which had been penetrated my foot like it was butter. The pain was searing and pulsating, and I nearly passed out. Fortunately, Joseph, Bob and Hen were at my side in a jiffy, and Joseph said, '*Una fanya nini*, what's wrong?'

I indicated my bloodied left foot and the huge thorn sticking out of my sole.

'*Pole rafikiangu. Pole*, I'm sorry my friend. I'm sorry,' Joseph muttered. 'Your brother has trodden on a terrible thorn. Now he will need some medicine,' Joseph addressed Bob and Hen. They nodded their heads in agreement, and commiserated with me as I lay beside the boulder in a bloodied, crumpled mess.

It was then that a tall and slightly gangling figure appeared over the brow of the parched and stony hill, wearing a white Muslim cap on his head, walking with a wooden staff and carrying a leather pouch at his waist.

'*Marahaba watoto*, greetings,' the stranger addressed us.

'*Shikamo mzee*, greetings, Sir,' we responded.

'*Hujambo, Baba mdogo,*' Joseph addressed his uncle, Hamid.

'*Sijambo, mpwa,* hello, nephew,' Hamid replied.

'*Una fanya nini*, what's up?' Hamid asked.

Joseph proceeded to tell Hamid everything that had happened, at which point he reached into his leather pouch and brought out a bunch of leaves, which he instructed me to apply to the wound caused by the thorn in my foot. With great deliberation and an intensely furrowed brow, I slowly removed the giant thorn, and began rubbing the leaves gently around the wound and swelling.

After a short while, the pain subsided and I felt immensely relieved and grateful to this *Hakim Mwislamu*, Muslim healer. It was the second time that I had personally seen the power of indigenous healing, whether through the spirit or plants.

Chapter Fifty-Three
Edward Kingston Farm, Nyeri,
31 December 1958

The clamorous bell rang out over the fields where the labourers had been sweltering over the harvesting of the maize crop at Kingston Farm, and the smears of red sandstone on their perspiring torsos and faces looked Hades-like in the dying rays of the African sun. The dromedary cattle had been dipped and then corralled for the night, and a soft, mellow sweetness was creeping into the russet twilight accompanied by the sounds of village women preparing for the evening meal.

Out of the corner of my eye, I saw Juma greeting an exhausted cyclist sent from Kitale Post Office with an urgent telegram. After a payment was exchanged, Juma walked briskly to the corner of the field where I was standing and issuing instructions about the maize storage.

'*Bwana*. A telegram for you.'

'*Asante sana*, Juma.'

'*Hata kidogo, Bwana.*'

I remove my penknife from my khaki shorts and proceed to open the telegram. It is stamped with a Cape Town postmark. I read:

Date: 22 December, 1958
To: Judge Edward Stephens STOP
Your wife taken seriously ill on board ship STOP Being flown to London for diagnostic tests STOP Children en route for Mr and Mrs Haines STOP Rathmines Dublin STOP
ENDS
British Consulate, Cape Town.

I stand rooted in front of Juma, who respectfully turns his gaze away from my anguished face.

'Take…er…take charge of the maize storage, Juma. *tafadhali*.'

'*Ndio, Bwana*.'

I turn slowly on my heels, still holding the telegram in both hands, and feel as if I've been struck a blow to the back of my head. Launching myself forward awkwardly, I curse under my breath.

'Diagnostic tests. Indeed.'

I painfully recall Izzy's recent bout of illness and my conversation with Dr Williams, our general practitioner about a month ago.

'*I'm afraid to say, Ted that your wife is suffering from a serious health condition. From what I cannot…*'

'*Just tell me the truth, Dr Williams. That's all I want to know.*'

'*Unfortunately, Ted, we can't carry out the necessary medical tests in Nairobi General Hospital, so…*'

'*Why's that?*'

'*It's just that the general hospital doesn't have the required consultant specialist to give a definitive diagnosis, and…*'

'*Frankly, Dr Williams, can't you at least give me your professional opinion?*'

'*In my opinion, I think your wife's best chance requires her immediate transfer to the Hospital for Tropical Medicine and Diseases…in London.*'

'*Er…and can you arrange this, Dr Williams?*'

'*I'll arrange it straight away, Edward, so rest assured.*'

'*Thanks, I appreciate that.*'

'*I'm sorry; Edward, but I will try and expedite matters as quickly as I can.*'

'*Thank you, Dr Williams. Goodbye.*'

As I shut the door behind Dr Williams, I'm in two minds as to whether or not I should tell Izzy any of this distressing news. But I feel I have no choice in the matter and walk upstairs to our bedroom.

'*So, my darling, what did Dr Williams have to say?*' *Izzy asks me, her voice quite faint.*

'*Ah…he said that you'll need some more blood tests to be taken in hospital…*'

'*Will I have to go away, Ted? Tell me the truth…*'

'*I…I'm afraid so, my dearest…*'

'And what about the children?'

'I'll speak to Charles and Edwina, darling, so don't worry about a thing...'

'I can't face leaving them, Ted, I really can't,' Izzy says, weeping uncontrollably.

'Please don't upset yourself, Izzy, just rest. It'll be all right, I promise you...'

'Oh, Ted, I can't bear it anymore,' Izzy says finally, breaking down in tears.

By some miracle, Izzy recovered enough to come out of Nairobi Hospital and persuaded me and Dr Williams that she could make her own way by boat to Dublin for Christmas where the boys could be properly cared for by her family in Rathmines.

Well, this telegram is the result of that decision.

I have a sudden flash of the sad and tearful faces of Izzy, Robert, Henry and Stan as they set off from Kingston Farm en route to Mombasa via Nairobi at the beginning of their journey to Dublin and the boys' grandparents in Rathmines. It was their tear-stained faces. That's what did it.

Yet Izzy's beautiful blue eyes were somehow vacant before she left for Nairobi with the boys. She kept looking into the horizon, as though she was looking for a way out, avoiding my gaze. And now there's this cable from Cape Town and suddenly my life is hanging by a silk thread.

Chapter Fifty-Four
Isabel Royal Brompton Hospital,
20 April 1959

It's a warm spring day, and the cherry blossom trees lining Brompton Road confidently announce winter's retreat. Robins and song thrushes compete for nesting materials while the busy commuters, taxis and red buses jostle for their place in London's fast pace.

Amidst the sounds and smells of hospital plumbing, surgical spirit and half-eaten hospital meals, I'm lying pale, thin and high on a chipped enamel bed staring intently at the spire of the Carmelite Church in the Fulham Road. I'm remembering our home in Rathmines, Dublin, just before the outbreak of War when we were planning a picnic outing that glorious summer.

The warm spring sunshine was beaming through the south-facing kitchen window, and the smell of our clutch of daffodils was in the air.

'Will you pass the sliced pan now, Nuala?' Eileen asks.

'Here you are, Ma. Shall I butter it and you do the fillings?'

'That's right, Nuala, you butter the slices and I'll do the cheese and tomato fillings, and Izzy, why don't you slice some onion to add to it?'

'Okay, Ma, I'll do that.'

For the next ten minutes, there is a sense of concentrated teamwork as we all pull together to put the finishing touches to our eagerly anticipated picnic. We're all very excited and Ma's singing one of her favourite songs, Oh for the wings of a Dove, which she plays so beautifully on the piano.

'That's such a beautiful song, Ma, and you sing it so well,' I say.

'Now don't cod me, Izzy. Is there a special favour you'll be wanting from me now?'

'No, really, Ma, it's lovely, that's all,' I respond.

At that moment, Da puts his head around the kitchen door and asks with a mock irritable tone, 'With the time you're taking, ladies, is it a banquet you're preparing now?'

'You wisht your noise now, Pat, or you'll be having none of this fine picnic the girls and I have laboriously prepared.'

Suitably admonished, Pat retreats from the kitchen while we girls put the finishing touches to the picnic.

'Make sure everyone has a piece of fruit and a packet of potato chips, will you, Nuala?'

'Of course, Ma.'

Soon, the picnic was complete and each of us girls carried a share of it in a wicker basket covered with a white napkin. As Da didn't have a car, we prepared to meet the bus at the end of Charleston Avenue that would take us to O'Connell Street Railway Station where we intended to get the train to Sandy Mount, south of the Dublin Bay. As we walked to the bus stop, many of our neighbours greeted us cheerfully.

The timings were perfect, and Berna met up with us in town, as she had a part-time office job on Saturday mornings. I remember those days when O'Connell Street Railway Station was filled with billowing steam engines, and the sounds and sites of excited travellers planning to spend a pleasant day at the seaside to make up for the long-wet winter and spring we had just endured.

As we were jogging along on the train, I say to Berna, as she was the worldliest among us.

'Do you foresee yourself always living in Ireland, Berna?'

'Well, Izzy, there's no place like home, and I've got a job, so I'm lucky, ain't I?'

'Yes...but sometimes I get a feeling that I want to travel far away and see something of the wide world.'

Sensing my dissatisfaction or wanderlust, Berna asks me, 'What is it that you're looking for that you can't find here, Izzy.'

'It's just that sometimes I feel...trapped here and don't want to be so...circumscribed.'

'Now, Izzy, that's a big word for you! What exactly do you mean?'

The steam train was slowing down now, and we were pulling in to Killiney station.

'I just want to be free, Berna, and experience the world of other cultures.'

A number of passengers disembarked from the train, while others climbed aboard and we were soon on our way again.

'The thing is, Izzy, you have to be realistic,' said Berna. 'There's about to be a war in Europe, and to be honest with you, I would thinking small and local if I were you.'

'That's all very well for you, Berna, you've always been drawn to office work and your good at it, but I'm thinking I want to go to drama school, and maybe go into fashion modelling,' I reply.

'I don't want to put a dampener on your hopes, Izzy, but I really think the world isn't a safe place at the moment, and as Lao Tzu said, "the wise man stays at home".'

'But I'm not a wise man, ain't I?' I laugh in response.

Berna laughs and smiles with me.

Within a few minutes, we're approaching Sandy Mount station and Eileen summons us together loudly and gathering all our picnic baskets and fizzy drinks, which Da is carrying, we disembark from the train.

That sunny Saturday, we had all our familiar variety of activities ranging from hand ball, running competitions which Da umpired, kite-making and sand castle building, and this Saturday on Sandy Mount beach passed as blissfully and uneventfully as all the other happy occasions I can remember from my childhood in Dublin.

Just as I'm settling into my pleasant reveries, the nursing sister with her starched uniform approaches my bed with a trolley on which I see a steel kidney-shaped bowl, a hypodermic syringe, a bottle of disinfectant and cotton swabs. I begin to feel faintly nauseous and wonder that I have any blood left in me after all these blood lettings I'm having recently. I just wish I could have the boys around me now and I know I would feel so much better.

On my side table, there are a few pictures that Ma's sent me of the boys. They're standing in front of Ma and Da wearing their shorts and new primary school uniforms of the "Sacred Heart". My God, surely they're too young for school. Our lives in Kenya seem so very far away now.

After the nursing sister has done her blood-letting, I'm tired and I nod off to sleep and have a dream.

I'm playing "hop, skip and jump" with my four sisters in Charleston Avenue. The smell of rotting leaves, autumn rain and washing suds from the gutters is penetrating. I feel happy. And suddenly, I'm dancing the Tango and Francesco's face is close to mine. For a short and breathless moment, we are one in timeless passion. Warmth pervades my being.

'Que sera, sera, whatever the future will be,' I sing. And surely, it's possible for a woman to love two men? My ma and Da are sitting in the living room at Charleston Avenue, and my younger sisters are playing with their dolls' house. Ted's angry face appears. I've been found out and start weeping. Going on is a worthless struggle. I begin to let go. I need peace and forgiveness now. That's all.

Chapter Fifty-Five
Edward and Isabel The Royal Brompton
Hospital, 27 April 1959

As I walk up the Brompton Road, I look up and see an airliner flying towards Heathrow amidst spring lamb-like clouds. It feels strange yet good to be in London. I hope I'm not too late as I find myself almost cantering up the last few steps to the entrance of this Victorian edifice that slightly chills me with its grey granite appearance.

As soon I walk into the dingy entrance hall, I smell it: that unmistakable smell of carbolic disinfectant and stale hospital meals. I take a deep inhalation of the primroses I'm carrying for Izzy to alleviate my distressed sense of smell.

'I've come to see my wife, Mrs Isabel Stephens. Can you tell me which ward she's on?'

'Of course, Sir. Maple Ward. Through the swing doors, turn right and you'll find a lift to the third floor. Follow the signs,' the starched receptionist replies.

As I'm going up to the third floor in the lift, I try to tune into the crashing and whirring of the pulley gears. It's somehow more soothing than acknowledging that I'm only partly here. A part of me has already taken flight as I approach Izzy's sick bed at the end of an interminably dark and evil-smelling corridor.

There she is surrounded by a medley of drips and tubes that seem like parasitic tentacles sucking her dry. I can hardly remember what she last looked like when I witness this pale, emaciated shell. I can see it takes every fibre of her being to greet me with a wan smile.

'Darling Ted. My prayers have been answered. You brought me primroses. How kind.'

'How are you, my darling Izzy?'

'I'm fine.' Like hell, I think.

I grasp both of her angular hands in mine as anger knots my bowels.

'How've you been, Ted?'

'Bloody awful.' Heartbroken.

'What the hell are they doing to you, Izzy?' I splutter.

'It's the radiation, Ted. It's killing me from the inside.' Yes, I can see that.

I yank myself up from the chair by Izzy's bed.

'Please, Ted. Don't make a scene.'

Gripping the end of Izzy's bed, I feel as if I'm strangling these men in white coats with coiled snakes around their necks that surround her like angels of death.

'I'll do more than make a scene.' I'll murder someone.

'For God's sake, Ted. Calm down. How are the children?'

As I adjust the pillows to help Izzy get more comfortable, I see her sagging breasts and fleshless ribcage beneath the operating gown. Yet my blind rage gives way to tender, excruciating pain. I'm finally broken, but just hang on for her sake.

'They're…They're with your parents in Rathmines,' I stumble over my words.

'Will you promise me something, Ted?'

'Whatever you wish, my darling.' To bring you back to life and health.

'Will you always love and care for them?' It's you I love and care for, my beloved Izzy.

'Of course, my darling,' I say with tears welling in my eyes.

Izzy starts to cry. I hold her bony frame close to mine. She's as light and ephemeral as a feather. And as I wipe the tears from her forehead and comfort her momentarily, I see a familiar glow in her eyes. It's the last happy memory I have of her at Stan's fourth birthday party, and as the guests are leaving, Robert and Henry rush on to the front lawn at Kingston Farm and thank everyone for coming.

The fading red flames of the African setting sun are disappearing in her blue eyes amidst her joyous laughs and scattered auburn curls. Her favourite aria, *"Libiamo"* from *"La Taviata"*, which I can hear somewhere inside me, serves as her final spirited refrain. That's Izzy. Not this.

'Please get me out of here, Ted. Please,' Izzy pleads, convulsed with sobs and nestling into my chest.

179

'I will. I promise you. I will,' I say, gritting my teeth.

I walk away from Izzy's bed and proceed to the sister's office at the end of this gloomy ward. The ward sister is short, rather stout and dressed in a blue and white uniform, and wears a smaller white cap than the other nurses. She looks at me quizzically.

'Can I help you, Mr Stephens?'

'Ah, hello, Sister. Do you mind if I have a quick word with you?'

'Of course, Mr Stephens. What can I do for you?'

'Well, I'm not sure how to put this, really, but in my opinion my wife's care is seriously deficient and...'

'What do you mean, "seriously deficient", Mr Stephens?'

'From what I can see for myself, Sister, my wife looks pale, sad and badly emaciated, and I'm afraid to say, I'm not happy with her treatment and care.'

'With all due respect, Mr Stephens, we are the professionals here and we are giving your wife the best possible treatment and care, so if you don't mind, I would prefer.'

'I do mind, Sister, and I insist on seeing the consultant responsible for her care.'

'Well, if that's the way you feel, Mr Stephens, I can arrange a meeting with him, if you like.'

'Can I meet with him now?'

'I'm afraid not, Mr Stephens, he's busy doing his ward rounds, but if you come back at ten o'clock tomorrow morning, I will arrange an appointment for you to speak to the consultant oncologist, Dr Carruthers.'

'Thank you, Sister, I appreciate that very much.'

'You're welcome, Mr Stephens. We look forward to seeing you tomorrow at ten o'clock.'

'Goodbye.'

'Goodbye.'

I eventually find my way out of that stinking maze of disinfected hospital corridors, and stumble out into the rush hour traffic of Brompton Road not knowing where I'm going, or why.

Chapter Fifty-Six
Go Physik to the Dogs The Royal Brompton Hospital, 28 April 1959

I arrive at the Royal Brompton Hospital at nine-forty-five, and am sheltering under my umbrella from a heavy shower and squally wind. As I walk into the entrance hall of the hospital, I address the receptionist.

'Good morning, Madam. Can you direct me to the office of Dr Carruthers, consultant oncologist?'

'Of course, Mr Stephens. Please take a seat. He's expecting you.'

As I sit in the rather drafy waiting area, I make a mental list of my complaints about Izzy's shambolic care. Sooner than I expected, Carruther's secretary comes to fetch me to his consulting room. As she shows me in to his pine panelled room, I get a clear picture of a rather ascetic, academic figure with thin, greying hair, a goatee beard and long, elegant fingers, which he stretches out to greet me.

'Ah, Mr Stephens. How nice to meet you! Do take a seat.'

'Thank you, Dr Caruthers,' I say, as I sit down opposite his rather formidable polished oak desk.

'I believe you are here to discuss your wife's care and treatment on Maple Ward, is that correct?'

'Exactly,' I respond.

'What exactly are your concerns, Mr Stephens?'

'To begin with, Dr Carruthers, I have never seen Isabel looking so drawn, emaciated and sad.'

'Well, you know, Mr Stephens, one of the difficult aspects of radiotherapy are these symptoms of weight loss, emaciation and loss of vitality. They are, alas, common side effects of the treatment.'

'I see, Dr Carruthers, but in all honesty, is this so-called treatment of yours doing her any good?'

'Of course, the radiotherapy is helping your wife, Mr Stephens. We wouldn't be doing it otherwise.'

'Is that so, Dr Carruthers? And so what is Isabel's diagnosis?'

'Well, it seems that the patient is suffering from some abnormal functioning of her thymus gland and we believe the growth it to be of a cancerous nature.'

'If you don't mind me asking, Dr Carruthers, where is the thymus gland?'

'Of course, Mr Stephens. The thymus gland sits in front of the thyroid gland on the external throat, about here,' he replies, indicating the place on his own throat.

'And what function does the thymus gland perform, Dr Carruthers?'

'It controls the body's immune function. That is, it's ability to combat disease, if you understand me?'

'I'm a lawyer by profession, Dr Carruthers, so these medical matters are a bit of a mystery to me, to be honest.'

'Of course, Mr Stephens, and that's why your wife is in the very best place in order to receive the most appropriate and professional treatment and care.'

'I see…And, can you tell me, Dr Carruthers, how long you expect the radiotherapy treatment will take to achieve the beneficial results you are seeking?'

'Well…that depends,' Carruthers says, as he strokes his goatee beard. 'The patient does seem to be having some benefit, from what the X-rays tell us, but I can't be sure how long, overall, her treatment will take.'

'I see…So I will have to leave these medical matters in your hands for the time being, Dr Carruthers.'

'I'm afraid so, Mr Stephens, but be assured, we are providing your wife with the most up-to-date medical protocol for this form of cancer, and you will have nothing to worry about, believe me.'

'I will have to take your word for it, Dr Carruthers. Unfortunately, I have to go back to Nairobi tomorrow, and I would appreciate it very much if you would keep me apprised of the progress of my wife's treatment and progress. Thank you. This is my card.'

As I hand Dr Carruthers my card, I look into his eyes and I see a confident and skilled medical practitioner, but someone who lacks a bedside manner.

'It has been good talking to you, Mr Stephens, and I can assure you that your wife is in safe hands with us at the Royal Brompton. Good morning.'

'Good morning, Dr Carruthers.'

As I walk out of the hospital, I try to gather my thoughts about what I have just heard and how I will convey the gist of it to dear Izzy. But I'm clear on one thing that I feel deeply and say within myself, 'Dr Carruthers, go physik to the dogs.'

After I have refreshed myself with a cup of coffee at the Lyons Tea House on Brompton Road, I pop into a grocers' store and buy a selection of tropical fruits to cheer Izzy up. Returning to the Royal Brompton to see her again on Maple Ward, I notice the sister-in-charge is different. The one I confronted yesterday is obviously off shift, thankfully.

As Izzy isn't expecting me at this time, I scrutinise her environment to get a sense if there have been any improvements to this rather dismal ward: there haven't. Izzy is lying unnaturally still, propped up in her bed with all those horrible parasitic lines going in and out of her, leaching out her life blood and vitality, I'm convinced.

'Izzy, my darling!'

'Oh, Ted, you surprised me!'

'Here you are, my darling, I've bought you some nice tropical fruits to feed you up, as well as remind you of Kenya.'

'Oh, bless you, Ted. How thoughtful of you!'

'You're most welcome, darling.'

As I'm arranging Izzy's fruit in a spare bowl, she asks me, 'Tell me, Ted, what did my consultant have to say?'

'Dr Carruthers told me that they are treating some sort of growth on your thymus gland with the radiation, which it seems to be responding to and...'

'But, Ted, I told you yesterday; it's killing me from the inside and I don't know if I...'

'Listen, Izzy, we have to trust that you're in the best place for the time being, and that the treatment is helping get rid of this damn thing.'

As I speak these words, I notice what little sparkle Izzy had in her eyes when I came in, slowly dwindles away. I'm mortified and helpless.

'I just wanted to say, Ted, in case I don't get the chance to say this to you: I'm truly sorry for what happened between Francesco and me and I thank you

for bringing Robert up as our own son. You have been truly magnanimous.'
Izzy starts to cry.

I reach over and hold her in my arms.

'I love you, Izzy, and I would do anything to bring you back to Kingston Farm and be a family again. I really would.'

When Izzy has recovered herself and dried her eyes, she says, 'When will you return and see me again, Ted?'

'I have to return to Nairobi tomorrow, but I will apply for more compassionate leave to return to your side as soon as I possibly can, my darling.'

'Thank you, and bless you, dear Ted. Return soon. I love you, always.'

'I love you, too, Izzy. Goodbye, or should I say *Au revoir*?'

'Goodbye, my darling. And give my love to the boys, won't you?'

'I will, my love. I will.' I'm not really in contact with them, now I think about it.

With those words, I turn away and try with all my remaining might to stem my tears which escape despite my best efforts. I exit this dismal hospital as soon as I can and make my way back to Elizabeth in Richmond to prepare for my departure for Kenya tomorrow.

Chapter Fifty-Seven
Betrayal Kingston Farm, 28 February 1960

It is late evening at Kingston Farm, and the servants have retired to their quarters, and all that remains to be done in the household can be accomplished by the three colleagues and friends sitting around a log fire in the living room. "Nyeri Triumvirate"—Judge Edward Stephens, Chief Inspector Mike Anderson and Charles Steel—are sitting around the fire nursing their half full tumblers of whisky.

'I'll tell you what, Charles, you tend to the fire a moment while I go and top up the carafe of whisky and water.'

'Okay, Ted, I'll do that,' says Charles, as he puts down his glass and moves towards the dwindling log fire. While loading the fire with logs and when Ted is in the kitchen topping up the carafe and water jug, Mike addresses Charles.

'So, Charles, how has Ted taken Isabel's death?'

'Badly, as you can expect. Very badly.'

'And to make matters worse, it turns out that the diagnosis and treatment were wrong, and by the time they discovered that, it was too later for poor Isabel,' says Charles.

'Yes, it was all very sudden, wasn't it?'

'My God! I can't imagine how traumatised Ted was to hear that,' says Mike.

'Absolutely, and to make matters worse, he's got three young boys to care for.'

'What will Ted do now, Charles?'

'He said to me he plans to send them to a boarding school in the south of England somewhere.'

At this juncture, Ted returns with the tray of whisky and water.

'Here we are, gentleman. This lot should see us through the evening nicely,' Ted says with a wide grin.

'Great, thanks, Ted,' Charles and Mike respond.

Once everyone has settled with their re-charged glasses of whisky and water, Ted opens the discussion.

'Right, gentlemen, what do you make of Prime Minister MacMillan's "Wind of Change" speech, then.'

'Well, if I can remember correctly, he gave the speech in South Africa earlier this month, much to the chagrin of the Nationalist Afrikaners, and to paraphrase it a little, he said something on the lines of: "the wind of change is blowing through Africa, and this growth of national consciousness is a political fact",' Mike says.

'You're spot on there, Mike,' Charles interjected.

'However, the point is, my friends, we have all been betrayed in deepest consequence by our political masters, to misquote Shakespeare, haven't we?' Ted says.

'That's absolutely right, Ted,' Mike responds.

'So were all our efforts and struggle to maintain power and influence in this colony completely wasted?' Ted asks.

'Yes, in short,' says Charles.

'It really beggars my belief in reason and common sense to see this cynical abandonment of our achievements and interests achieved over the last seventy-five years,' Ted says.

'I'm afraid to say, Ted, we have all had to live with the exigencies of "real politik",' interjects Mike.

'That's a fact,' concludes Charles.

'So what's your "exit strategy" going to be, Ted?' asks Mike.

'I've written to the chief justice and tendered my resignation, which is long overdue.'

'And when will that take effect, Ted?' Charles asks.

'In six months' time. I've got to wind matters up here first.'

'My God, this is all unravelling faster than I could ever have imagined,' says Mike.

'Well, Mike, it just goes to show, we were only "mere players on the stage of history, full of sound and fury, but signifying nothing", to misquote our Shakespeare again.'

"Well said; absolutely", Charles and Mike chorus in turn.

'And you, Charles, what are your plans?' Ted asks.

'I've discussed matters with Edwina, and we've decided to stay on a couple more years, for the sake of the children. And, frankly, with the prospect of no servants and the terrible British climate, you can't blame us, can you?' Charles replies, and everyone laughs.

'How about you, Mike?' Ted asks.

'I've decided to apply for a senior managerial post in the Met,' replies Mike.

'So who knows, gentlemen, in a year's time, the three of us will be scattered to the wind, like that damn MacMillan's speech predicted,' says Ted.

"Very apt; Absolutely", Charles and Mike respond in turns.

'Well, Ted, it's been a very pleasant evening and I'm sorry that there will be too few remaining for us, but I must be going now,' says Mike, draining his glass and standing up to leave.

'You're most welcome, my friend, and who knows, we might even have another glass of whisky together in Blighty sooner than we can imagine,' Ted responds.

Mike utters a wry laugh at this comment and makes his way to the front door, turning around before he leaves.

'Bye, Charles. I'll see you around before I go, I'm certain.'

'You bet you will, Mike. Goodbye.'

Before Charles gets up to leave, Ted beckons him to wait a while as he has something personal to discuss. Topping up Charles' glass, Ted says, 'I've been thinking, Charles…'

'About what, Ted?'

'About Mischief.'

'Your polo pony?'

'That's it. And I'm wondering if you would consider taking him on for me. Would you consider that, Charles?'

'Of course, I would, my friend, anytime.'

Edward's eyes film over with tears of relief as he hears this response, and Charles reaches out his arm and places it on Ted's.

'I…I can't thank you enough, Charles. This means more than I can say.'

'I know, old chap. I really do.'

'Thank you.'

Edward shows Charles to the front door of Kingston Farm and bids him farewell. Before he closes the front door, he calls Cleo and Rex to his side and walks outside with them.

'What do you think, Cleo and Rex? Are we all washed up here? Is it time to leave Kingston Farm?'

Cleo and Rex run back and forth between Ted and the bushes where they have already picked up the scent of a prowling hyena, which excites them both. Ted looks up at the carpet of diamond bright stars studding the Africa night sky and contemplates letting go of everything he's fought for in Kenya Colony for the very first time.

Chapter Fifty-Eight
Kwaheri Mischief Muthaiga
Polo Ground, 20 April 1960

It is a crisp, warm morning in Nairobi, and Edward is at the Muthaiga Polo Ground standing outside Mischief's stable. Mischief is surprised to see Edward at this unaccustomed hour of the morning and seems torn between pulling at his hay net or greeting his owner and rider.

'How have you been then, Mischief? Has Charles taken you out at all?'

Mischief whinnies and waves his head at Edward, in response.

Edward pulls the bolt to his stall and goes into his stable with the grooming kit that he's holding in his left hand. While Mischief is chewing away contentedly, Edward begins to give him a thorough grooming. As he does so, he begins to remember the first pony called "Mischief" that he ever owned.

I saw him. He's white, about thirteen hands with a long white mane and an intelligent-looking face and eyes. I can't quite believe my luck, as I take delight in his pawing impatience and cheeky Welsh mountain stance.

'Dad, over there. Look, can you see the white pony?' I said as I pulled Dad by his hand towards the pony pen.

'All right, Eddie, let's take a closer look at him, shall we?' He said as we approached the pen.

As we viewed the Connemara ponies with their long hair, stout hind quarters, and long rough manes, both our eyes were drawn towards the white Welsh mountain pony whose gaze met mine. As I began to tune into his strong presence, he began to approach me in a confident manner, almost as if he had known that I was coming all along. Finally, he stopped in front of the temporary wooden fencing and raised his long, muscled neck towards my face.

I was a little surprised but stood my ground. Noticing my confidence, he breathed into my face, and that warm stream of hay and bran-laden breath filled my lungs with its sweetness and magic. I was truly enraptured with him.

Trance-like, I breathed, 'Isn't he lovely, Dad?'

'Yes, he's a fine-looking stallion,' my father chuckled good-humouredly, and scratched his head. 'Let's find out what the dealer hopes to get for him.'

We set off hand-in-hand towards the knot of smartly-dressed dealers in their trench coats, boots and tweeds. My father soon established who the owner of the pony was and I observed his shrewd manner and reticent speech. I feared he might want a high price for him. And soon we were all gathered round the pen.

'Oh no, Dad, I hope he's not going to be too expensive,' I fretted as my father put his reassuring hand on my shoulder and assumed his poker face. The auctioneer started the bidding off.

'Can we start with thirty guineas, gentlemen?'

A hand to our left was slightly raised.

'Forty I'm bid over there. Anyone for fifty?'

I squeezed Dad's left hand and he raised his right.

'That's good, fifty over here now. Any improvement on that?'

I whispered a silent "Hail Mary".

'Sixty. Excellent,' he said, indicating a portly farmer opposite.

'Can I confirm sixty guineas to the gentleman over there?'

I gave Dad my very tightest squeeze and made a silent covenant to sacrifice a month's pocket money if Dad bid higher. He did.

'Sixty-five it is then, over here. Confirming sixty-five guineas over here.'

And just as I thought Mother Mary had interceded for me, the auctioneer called out, 'That's seventy guineas to the gentleman over there,' as he indicated the portly farmer once again.

In desperation, I made a silent covenant of two month's pocket money, and prayed to Mary again as I squeezed Dad's hand with all my remaining strength. As I began to feel weak at the knees, I just caught the tail end of the auctioneer's last words.

'Going, going, gone to Colonel Stephens at seventy-five guineas.'

I gave Dad my biggest ever hug, burying my head in his cavalry twills.

'Thanks, Dad; he's the best birthday present in the world.'

'Well, dear Mischief, you do remind me so much of your namesake back in Kildare, you really do.'

Mischief pushed Edward away playfully, while also sensing he had something more to say.

'So, dear Mischief, it's time to say *kwaheri* and goodbye, my beloved treasure.'

Edward held Mischief with his face against his warm neck and his right hand on his withers for a long time and just listened to his quiet rhythmic breathing. He felt he could have stayed longer, but the tears started to come and rather than distress his pony, he picked up the grooming kit and closed the stable door behind him. As he walked away, the sound of Mischief's whinnies receded into the distance.

Chapter Fifty-Nine
Kwaheri, Bwana Edward
Kingston Farm, Nyeri, 21 April 1960

Edward took his rifle off the stand above the fireplace and went to the chest of drawers opposite the French windows overlooking the parched and patchy brown lawn of Kingston Farm. He opened a small drawer, carefully loaded two cartridges into the breach. Opening the patio doors, he called Cleo and Rex. Puzzled by his unusual expression, the two dogs followed him obediently into the adjoining yard.

They stirred restlessly as if they could read his intentions. Edward tried to calm them both with reassuring words and gestures. In order to accomplish his task, he tethered them both to the wooden fence surrounding the patio. Eventually, they settled down and looked at him with dumb trust.

He took careful aim at each of them in turn and discharged both barrels. First Cleo, then Rex went down without a whimper. For a shocked and reverberating moment, there was complete silence. Edward stood transfixed holding the rifle and then sank to his knees covering his face with his hands. He remained motionless for what seemed an eternity.

Dark red pools of blood began to coagulate around the smashed heads of his two faithful friends. And then the flies began to do their work. The enormity of what he had just done made Edward nauseous. He wiped his brow and eyes with his handkerchief. He tried to stand. It was impossible. Sinking to his knees again, he started to weep and shake uncontrollably.

'Juma!' He shouted. Juma had run to the rear of the house on hearing the shots and had been observing this bizarre scene from behind a tree in disbelief. Stemming his tears, Edward said, '*Waumbwa*...Bury the dogs, Juma, *tafadhali.*'

'*Ndio, Bwana,*' he replied.

Juma walked over to him and did something he had never done before. He laid both his hands on *Bwana* Edward's shoulders. Edward didn't resist his touch.

'*Ku-saidia mimi*, Juma. Help me.'

Juma took *Bwana* Edward by his right arm and gently helped him to his feet. He staggered and swayed for a few moments, but Juma held firm.

'*Waumbwa.* Bury the dogs, Juma,' Edward said.

'*Kuchelewa, Bwana*, later,' Juma replied.

Slowly, Juma led *Bwana* Edward inside the living room and guided him into his settee. Gradually, regaining his senses, Edward said, 'Whisky *tafadhali*, Juma. Pour me whisky.'

'*Ndio, Bwana*,' Juma replied.

A few moments later, Juma returned with a glass, a carafe of whisky and a jug of water.

'Does *Bwana* Edward want something more?' Juma asked.

'*Waumbwa,* bury the dogs, Juma, *tafadhali*,' Edward said.

'*Ndio kabisa*, yes, surely,' Juma replied.

'*Asante sana*, thank you, Juma. *Vizuri usiku,* good night.'

'*Vizuri usiku, Bwana*.'

As he swallowed his whisky, he looked out through the French windows and into the distance where the black line of the forest was giving way to a fading blue and gold African sky. The sudden twilight and galloping onset of night was being ushered in by a growing chorus of crickets and tree frogs in this forsaken outpost of disintegrating empire. Edward's gaze shifted from the horizon as he reached over to switch on the standard lamp.

On the top of his open bureau, there was a picture of Izzy, reclining on the lawn with Cleo beside her, Robert lying with his black head of hair resting on Cleo's shoulder, a curly, blonde, Henry with his legs in the air, and Stan reclining in the muslin-covered cot. He reached up to the bureau, grasped the silver-framed picture, placed it in his lap and stared at it for a long while.

Slowly his head nodded, coming to a resting position on his chest. Edward sank into a dream of his first meeting with Izzy selling primroses outside Trinity College, Dublin.

I'm standing close to Izzy, fingering my bowler hat nervously as she tries to secure the primrose in my buttonhole, laughing girlishly all the while. Her clear, blue eyes make a startling contrast to her auburn hair. I feel awkward

193

and anxious. But I'm radiant inside. After all, she's the first girl I've ever really desired. It's almost unbearable. I reach out to touch her and I see her with her secret lover, Francesco, with his sinewy arms around her waist. They are kissing and laughing.

'You're so exciting, Isabel. How can you think of marrying him?'

'He's loyal, aristocratic and kind. How could I do anything to hurt his feelings?'

'Is that so?'

I feel as though I've been stabbed in the chest. I can't breathe.

'Izzy!' Edward cried out in his sleep.

'Why?'

His voice echoed around the room. The perspiration on his brow was streaming down his neck. He gasped for air. How could I have ever trusted her with my love? She betrayed me utterly. I was a fool. As he adjusted to the bright yellow gleam of light that illuminated the living room, his gaze rested on a pile of toys, a drum, an incomplete jigsaw, a cowboy suit and a red tricycle. Breathing erratically, he reached over to the tray and poured himself another whisky.

Finally, it dawned on him. Izzy and the boys were finally gone from his life and home.

Sometime later, Juma came back into the living room quietly. As he approached *Bwana* Edward's settee, he noticed him asleep with an empty carafe of whisky by his elbow and a family portrait in his lap. Juma placed the photograph carefully back on the bureau, turned the standard lamp off, and covered *Bwana* Edward with a blanket as the sounds of tree frogs and crickets reached a crescendo outside Kingston Farm.

Chapter Sixty
Wazungu Wenda, Asante Ngai
The Europeans Are Going, Thank God

Mzee, the wrinkled shaman, looks at each of the tribal elders round the circle enshrouded in the smoke of bang, hemp, and walks to the central clearing in the compound. He addresses them all in Gikuyu 'I am pleased to say that the *wazungu* are now going from our land. This is a good sign. The *Gethathi*, curse, can now be lifted, and all transgressions forgiven.'

Another of the elders responds, 'And what about *Bwana* judge, Mzee?'

The shaman rises to his full stature and says, '*Bwana* judge and his family are also leaving, and taking our *Malaika* with them.'

He then begins to intone the words of an ancient lore, while he proceeds to cut the throat of the goat which is tethered at his feet. Apart from suffocating, guttural cries and shaking, the goat doesn't struggle. The shaman's knife pierces its carotid artery and the blood begins to flow in jerking torrents.

He captures the goat's blood in a gourd and begins to offer it around the circle of elders. Each of them drinks, and gives thanks with the words "*wazungu wenda, tha thaya Ngai,* the Europeans are leaving, thank God".

The sound of the rhythmic *ngoma,* drum, drifts over the trees, mingling with the mists of the impenetrable forest below.